MY LiFe
as a
Blundering
Ballerina

BOOKS BY BILL MYERS

The Incredible Worlds of Wally McDoogle (18 books)
—*My Life As a Smashed Burrito with Extra Hot Sauce*
—*My Life As Alien Monster Bait*
—*My Life As a Broken Bungee Cord*
—*My Life As Crocodile Junk Food*
—*My Life As Dinosaur Dental Floss*
—*My Life As a Torpedo Test Target*
—*My Life As a Human Hockey Puck*
—*My Life As an Afterthought Astronaut*
—*My Life As Reindeer Road Kill*
—*My Life As a Toasted Time Traveler*
—*My Life As Polluted Pond Scum*
—*My Life As a Bigfoot Breath Mint*
—*My Life As a Blundering Ballerina*
—*My Life As a Screaming Skydiver*
—*My Life As a Human Hairball*
—*My Life As a Walrus Whoopee Cushion*
—*My Life As a Mixed-Up Millennium Bug*
—*My Life As a Beat-Up Basketball Backboard*

Other Children's Series
McGee and Me! (12 books)
Bloodhounds, Inc. (8 books)

Teen Series
Forbidden Doors (10 Books)

Teen Nonfiction
Hot Topics, Tough Questions
Faith Encounter

Picture Book
Baseball for Breakfast

Adult Fiction
Blood of Heaven
Threshold
Fire of Heaven
Eli

Adult Nonfiction
Christ B.C.
*The Dark Side of
Supernatural*

www.Billmyers.com

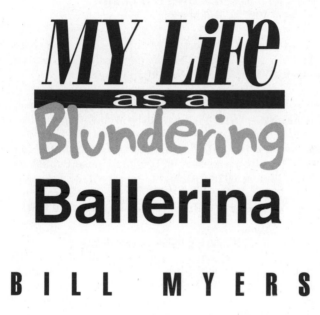

MY LiFe as a Blundering Ballerina

BILL MYERS

Tommy
NELSON®

Thomas Nelson, Inc.
Nashville

Published in Nashville, Tennessee, by Tommy Nelson®, a division of Thomas Nelson, Inc. Visit us on the Web at tommynelson.com

Verses marked TLB are taken from *The Living Bible,* copyright © 1971. Used by permission of Tyndale House Publishers, Inc., Wheaton, Illinois, 60189. All rights reserved.

Library of Congress Cataloging-in-Publication Data

Myers, Bill, 1953–
   My life as a blundering ballerina / Bill Myers.
      p.   cm. — (The incredible worlds of Wally McDoogle ; bk. 13)
   Summary: At the suggestion of their speech teacher, Wally and his good friend Wall Street agree to switch places for three days to prove whether boys or girls are better.
   ISBN 0–8499–4022–2
   [1. Sex role—Fiction. 2. Christian life—Fiction.
3. Humorous stories.] I. Title. II. Series: Myers, Bill, 1953–   .
Incredible worlds of Wally McDoogle ; #13.
PZ7.M98234Mydd   1997
[Fic]—dc21
                                                      97–34366
                                                          CIP
                                                           AC

Printed in the United States of America

02 03 04 PHX 12 11 10

For Bill Myers, Sr.—
one of my heroes.

Love each other with brotherly
affection and take delight in
honoring each other.

—Romans 12:10 (TLB)

Contents

Chapter 1

Just for Starters . . .

"It's way harder being a guy than a girl."

"Is not."

"Is too."

"Is not."

"Is too."

The best thing about this kind of argument is that it can go on forever.

"Is not."

"Is too."

"Is not."

"Is too."

I mean it's so mindless you can pick up a good book (preferably something with a title that starts with "My Life As . . ."), or catch an *America's Funniest Home Videos* rerun, or even do complex fractions—all at the same time—and still keep it going.

"Is not."

"Is too."

"Is not."

"Is too."

Unfortunately Wall Street, my best friend (even if she is a girl), and I were just getting into it when Ms. Finglestooper strolled over. As our drama and speech teacher and a recent graduate of Fruitcake U (or some other weird college out West), she felt it was her solemn duty to make every minor mole-hill into a major mountain.

"Wally," she said, "I think you and Wall Street might have a topic for some speeches here." Before we could answer, she turned to the rest of the class and called, "People! People, gather around here for a moment."

And since "gather around" sounded a lot better than "sit in your seat, keep quiet, and do your work," the class immediately obeyed.

"What's up?" they asked as they crowded around us.

"Well, Wally here thinks being a young man is tougher than being a young woman. And Wall Street believes it's just the opposite." She turned to us. "Is that correct?"

Wall Street and I nodded our heads off. So did the rest of the class . . . the boys agreeing with me, the girls with Wall Street. And before we knew it, the entire class had returned to the debate:

"Is not."

"Is too."

"Is not."

"Is—"

"Class . . . class . . ." Ms. Finglestooper clapped her hands. "I think there's a way to settle this argument a little more intelligently, and maybe create some interesting speeches at the same time."

"How's that?" I asked. (Unfortunately I had not read the back cover to this book, otherwise I would have kept quiet and run for my life.)

Ms. Finglestooper smiled. "All you two need to do is simply trade places."

"What do you mean?" Wall Street asked.

"You and Wally agree to live each others' lives for a certain amount of time. Let's say, seventy-two hours."

"What?!" we cried in unison.

"Sure . . . it will be perfect." She pointed to me. "You'd get a taste of what girls go through, and you," she pointed to Wall Street, "will become more sensitive to what guys face. Then, when it's all over, you may both present speeches about what you've learned."

"I don't know," Opera, my other best friend, said. "I'm not so sure how Wally will look in a dress."

The class snickered, but Ms. Finglestooper shook

her head. "No, no, we won't go to that extreme, but—"

One of the guys interrupted. "Wall Street couldn't last ten minutes as a guy."

"She'd last longer than Wally as a girl," someone argued.

"Would not."

"Would too."

"Would not."

It was nice to hear the discussion getting back to normal. But, unfortunately, as we all know, "normal" never lasts too long in my neck of reality.

Then I heard, "Hey, I gots a gooder idea." By the stunning lack of grammar everyone knew it was Bruce Breakaface, our star football player, talking. "Let's, uh, turns it into like a competition—guys against girls. Yeah, and whoever gives in first, uh . . . ," he frowned as he tried to concentrate. "Uh . . ."

"Loses," somebody whispered.

Suddenly his face lit up. "Yeah . . . whoever gives in first loses."

"A piece of cake!" The guys shouted. "You girls are history!"

"No way!" The girls yelled back. "You guys are dead meat!"

"Well," Ms. Finglestooper said, "now that we've covered most of the major food groups, let's spend the rest of the period writing down the ground rules so everything will be fair and square."

"All right!" The guys yelled.

"Cool!" The girls shouted.

But not me. It's hard to yell anything when you're busy having your body shoved against the wall by one Mr. Bruce Breakaface. He didn't say much. He didn't have to. I could sense it by the glare in his eyes . . . and his choke hold around my throat.

"Don't let *us* down, McDoogle," he said.

I understood perfectly. The *us* was every guy that had ever lived . . . especially Bruce Breakaface. And the *letting down* would be if I lost to Wall Street. The message couldn't be clearer— I could either win or I could die.

* * * * *

"So how are they gonna make sure you do all the girlie stuff?" Burt, one of my twin older brothers, asked. He was gnawing on a piece of German sausage. Well, it was supposed to be German sausage. But since it was Wednesday night, and our little sister Carrie's turn to make dinner, the outside tasted and chewed more like bicycle tires . . . with an inside full of something like overcooked kitty litter. (Carrie still hadn't mastered the fine art of cooking.)

"We're going to have judges," I said as I secretly loaded up my napkin with another one of my sister's gourmet treats—mashed potatoes that had the delicate taste and aroma of boiled clay.

"So people are gonna follow you around?" Brock, my other brother, asked.

I nodded. "Starting first thing tomorrow morning, different kids will be watching Wall Street and me." I carefully eased the potatoes below the table and held them out to Collision, our family cat. Having the IQ of a stump, ol' Collision gobbled them down like there was no tomorrow. And, given the toxic nature of Carrie's cooking, that just might be the case.

"Pass the glue," Burt asked.

"That's not glue!" Carrie protested. "It's gravy."

"Yeah, right," he smirked. "If that's gravy then I suppose these hard little BB thingamabobs are corn."

"Peas," Carrie corrected. "I just fried them a little too long."

Mom pretended to cough into her napkin (although I secretly suspected she was also preparing a treat for Collision). "Actually, green peas are supposed to be boiled, sweetheart, not fried."

"Oh. Even after I've marinated them in hot sauce?"

Now everybody was coughing into their napkins.

"I don't know," Dad said to me when he finally came up for air. "Trading places with a girl? You don't think that's going to sissify or warp you, do you?"

"Not any more than he's already warped," Burt snickered.

I threw a cautious look to Dad. After all, his idea of being a man involves arm wrestling Arnold Schwartzenegger, being a professional linebacker, and picking my teeth with ten-inch iron nails—all at the same time. In fact, it seems like whenever I turn around lately, he's shoving a hockey stick or weightlifting magazines into my hands.

"Oh, relax, Herb," Mom said cheerfully. "I think it will be great fun. Besides, I'm sure it will help the boys and girls be a little more understanding of each other."

Dad gave a long sigh. "Well, all right," he grumbled, "just as long as he doesn't have to wear a dress or anything."

"No way," I laughed. "You wouldn't catch me in anything like that."

"Well actually . . ." Mom hesitated.

We all looked at her.

"Actually, what?" I asked. (Suddenly wishing I'd read the back cover of this book, again.)

"Well, doesn't *The Nutcracker* ballet open the day after tomorrow?"

"Yeah."

"And isn't Wall Street playing the part of the Sugar Plum Fairy?"

"So?"

"So, if you two are supposed to be trading places for seventy-two hours and the ballet is in forty-eight . . ." She let the phrase trail off.

I tried to answer, but it's hard to talk when you're hyperventilating.

"You mean Wally's going to have to be in a ballet?" Carrie asked in wide-eyed amazement.

Suddenly Burt broke out in laughter, followed by Brock.

"Way to go Wally!" Burt slapped me on the back. (Or was it Brock?)

"Cool," Brock snickered. (Or was it Burt?)

I threw another glance to Dad, who looked almost as bad as I felt. Something about seeing his little boy in a tutu and tights made him majorly uncomfortable.

It didn't help my comfort level much either.

But before Dad could reach for the phone and enlist me in the Marine Corps or at least sign me up as Evander Holyfield's boxing partner, Collision went into one of her major coughing fits.

We all turned and watched as the cat ran around and around the room coughing and howling.

"Oh no," little Carrie groaned. "Somebody call the vet. Collision is doing it again."

But the running only lasted a minute before it was interrupted by another routine—the one where the cat throws herself down on the floor and starts scooting around and around on her side. Next she starts jumping straight up into the air and then gravity pulls her down. Over and over, she goes straight up into the air and then down.

"Amazing," little Carrie shook her head. "Whenever it's my night to cook she does the exact same thing. I wonder why?"

I glanced around to the rest of the family. Everyone was quietly bringing their napkins back up from under the table and silently setting them beside their plates. Poor Collision. It looked like once again she was the only one eating my sister's cooking.

Fortunately, the little diversion had distracted Dad from calling the Marines. Unfortunately it did little to solve my upcoming stroll through another McDoogle mishap.

Chapter 2

Bumble Boy to the Rescue

Most people count sheep when they can't go to sleep. Not me. I was counting how many places Bruce Breakaface's fists were going to land on me. And when I got tired of that, I started counting the number of trips to the Emergency Room I'd be making. It's not that I was scared or anything. It's just that if I lost the competition with Wall Street every guy in the world would be humiliated beyond belief. Of course, that would include Bruce Breakaface, who, as you've probably figured out, did not get his name by accident.

I knew I could beat Wall Street—after all, she was just a girl. Right? I figured all I had to do was scream at every little crawly thing, call every guy I met "immature," and flick my hair out of my eyes a zillion times. That's all there was to this girl stuff.

But there was still that one in a billion chance that something might go wrong. Or, in my case, that something might go right. So, I reached for Ol' Betsy, my laptop computer. Nothing takes my mind off an upcoming death sentence like writing a good superhero story.

It has been another long day of heroics for the world famous (and part-time telemarketing salesman) Bumble Boy. He's defused a terrorist's bomb, invented a cure for watching too many TV reruns, and telephoned the same household five times asking if they wanted to change from one phone company to another.

And now he is hanging up his wings, kicking off his shoes (all six of them), and sitting down with a plate of chocolate chip pollen and a nice cold glass of nectar.

No one knows how Bumble Boy turned into half-bee, half-boy, but it sure gets expensive when he's shopping for clothes. (Ever try talking your mom into buying three pairs of Air Jordans at the same time?)

Then there's the little stinger problem. Granted, it stops people from shoving

behind him in line, but it definitely
makes sitting on air mattresses and
water beds a little tricky.

But on with our story. Our stunningly
sensational and sometimes sticky superhero (say that seven times fast) is just
opening up his latest issue of *Better
Beehives and Gardens* when suddenly the
Bumble Phone rings

> *BZZZ-BZZZ-BZZZ.*
> *BZZZ-BZZZ-BZZZ.*

He scoops up the phone with one of his
six legs and answers: "Superheros,
Unlimited: If needing to be saved is
your thing, I'm the bee with the sting."

At first there is no answer.

"Hello—"

Then finally, through muffled static,
he hears a dreaded voice:

> "Alas, poor Bug Boy,
> We doth meet again.
> But things shall be different,
> This time I'll do *you* in."

The phrase sends a cold chill through
our hero's exoskeleton. (Do bees have

exoskeletons? Well, this one does.)
Immediately he recognizes the voice. It
belongs to none other than (insert scary
music here)...Shakespeare Guy!

"Shakespeare Guy," our hero shouts.
"Shakespeare Guy, is that you?"

"Alas, what knowledge,
Through your thick skull
        doth break.
Thou doth not speak a lie,
'Tis indeed the sensational 'I'."

Bumble Boy shudders a shuddering
shudder of recognition. Of course it's
Shakespeare Guy. Who else could speak
such bad poetry? "But how——how did you
get out?" Bumble Boy asks. "You were
serving a life sentence in a mental hospital for the artistically insane."

"A wondrous potion,
Hath I concocted.
Then gave it to my warden,
So my sentence he hath forgotten."

Bumble Boy cringes. He remembers all
too well the torture this fiendish
fiend had once inflicted upon the

world. How literature teachers had dropped to their knees begging him to stop reciting his verses. How poets had gone insane listening to his work. And how (after Bumble Boy had captured him) he was sentenced to life without parole for Cruel and Unusual Punishment of the English Language.

But how was it possible? Had he really escaped? Was he really on the telephone? Was Bumble Boy really talking to him? (Could our superhero think of any more lame questions to ask before continuing our story?)

"Are you serious?" Bumble Boy cries. (Well, I guess we have our answer, don't we?) "Did you really invent some sort of potion?"

> "Thou has stated it wisely,
> And now shall I reveal my quest.
> I've slipped it into the world's
>   water,
> So what dost thou think, insectoid
>   breath?"

"But what does it do?" our hero cries. "What type of effect does the potion have upon people?"

"Just snappeth on your remote,
If thou dost really want to know.
Flippeth on any channel,
And watcheth any show."

Bumble Boy reaches for his TV remote while talking with Shakespeare Guy, drinking his nectar, munching his chocolate chip pollen, and scratching behind his left antenna. (Having six legs does have some advantages—you should see him brush, floss, gargle, and play the saxophone at the same time.)

At last the picture comes on the TV and Bumble Boy gasps a superhero gasp. It's another *Brady Bunch* rerun (no surprise there—just try turning on TV without seeing one). But instead of Marsha, Greg, and all the gang speaking 1970s polyester style talk, they're all speaking...Shakespearean!

"Forsooth, O gentle Marsha,
Methinks thou dost have
An unseemly zit,
Upon the tip of thy nostril."

"Nay, Greg, tell me 'tis not so."

"Alas and alack.
Test me not, tender Marsha.
For a zit by any other name
Is still a—"

In a panic, Bumble Boy switches channels. It is another rerun:

"Ayeee, Ritchie...
I speaketh to thee a dare
If thy wants they nose broketh,
Just messeth with Fonzie's hair."

Again Bumble Boy switches channels.
This time to a big yellow bird hopping
around with a bunch of children singing:

"Can thou tellest me how
To proceed to Sesame—"

Bumble Boy can stand no more. He turns
off the TV and shouts into the phone:
"This is insane!"

"Thou hast stated it correctly,
Though thou needest not be sad.
For there's still a way to
      stop me,

```
From making English
Sound so bad."
```

```
"What do I do?! Tell me, what do I have
to do?"
```

```
"Meetest me in New York City,
The World Trade Center, I suggest.
Where we'll duel for the potion,
Till I squisheth thee dead,
You insectoid pest!"
```

```
Bumble Boy groans. The poetry is get-
ting worse. He hangs up the telephone
and dashes for the door. He knows he
must help. That's what he has to do.
He must putteth a stop to this torture.
Oh no! 'Tis affecting him, too!
```

That was enough for one night. Actually more
than enough. I saved the file and shut Ol' Betsy
down. It was a pretty good story. I just hoped I'd
be alive to finish it.

* * * * *

The next thing I remember, I was in the middle

of a giant earthquake with all of the standard earthquake features—you know, the shaking room, shaking bed, shaking me. And what catastrophe would be complete without yelling. Lots and lots of yelling. But instead of coming from me (which is usually the case) it came from someplace entirely different.

"Okay, McDoogle! Let's get up now! Rise and shine. Come on, McDoogle, wake up! Don't want to be late for your first day of competition!"

It almost sounded like one of the girls from my speech class.

"Wow, he looks even dorkier asleep than when he's awake!"

Now I knew it was somebody from my class.

My eyes exploded open. But this was no earthquake, it was an invasion! Not one, but *two* girl types were standing directly over my bed! They were the ones shaking me and trying to wake me up.

"What are you doing here?" I cried.

"Your mom let us in," the first said as she pushed up her glasses and gave a loud sniff. It was Francine Dripplenose, our local genius. She had an IQ higher than the moon and a nonstop case of allergies.

"That's right."

I turned to the other voice. It was Sylvia

Wisenmouth, our school's shining hope as a future gold medalist—just as soon as they create an Olympic event for smart alecks. "It's time to start the competition, McMutant."

I fumbled for my glasses and looked to the radio alarm. "It's only five thirty in the morning!"

"Yeah, we're running a little late," Sylvia said, yanking off the covers. (Fortunately I was wearing my *Batman* PJ's—my *Beauty and the Beasts* were still in the laundry.) "We've got to make up for lost time."

"Lost time? But school doesn't start until eight!"

"That is *sniff* correct," Francine said, wiping her nose with the back of her hand. "And for you to spend the mandatory *sniff* two-point-two hours in the bathroom, you had better *sniff* commence immediately."

"Two-point-two hours!"

"That's how long Wall Street has to spend on her hair every morning," Sylvia explained.

"That's crazy. I'm not going to do that!"

"Oh really?" she asked, lifting an eyebrow.

"Really," I said, crossing my arms.

"So are you forfeiting already?" she asked. "Are you admitting defeat and letting the girls win?"

I started to nod then suddenly remembered Bruce Breakaface. Well, not all of him, just the fists part. If I admitted defeat, I'd have to break the news to him. And after I broke the news, he'd break my face.

"Well . . . no," I hedged, "not exactly."

"Then get a move on!"

A moment later I was locked inside the bathroom. I did all my usual get-ready-for-school stuff. But after the 19 seconds had come and gone, I'd completely run out of things to do.

"Girls," I shouted, "I can't just stand here for over two hours. I need some suggestions."

"No problem," Francine called from the other side of the door. "As you may recall, *sniff* the average human head *sniff* contains 55,676 hair follicles."

"Of course," I lied. "Everybody knows that."

"So, *sniff-sniff* through simple mathematics, if you divide two-point-two hours by 55,676, you actually only have fourteen one-hundredths of a second to comb each strand of hair."

"Meaning?"

"Meaning," Ms. Calculator-For-A-Brain continued, "in the course of this nine-second discussion, you could have combed sixty-four point two hairs."

"So quit wasting time, McMoron," Sylvia bellowed, "and get to work!"

I wanted to argue more, but who knew how many other hairs I'd be leaving out in the process. So, without another word, I grabbed the comb and tried to make up for lost time.

It was 7:42 when I finally staggered out of the bathroom. Every strand of hair was perfect, but my stomach was starved. I turned and started toward the kitchen where I could already smell Mom's bacon and eggs. But, suddenly, Sylvia blocked my path.

"Where do you think you're going?" she demanded.

"Breakfast."

"No way."

"What?"

"Wall Street *sniff* doesn't eat breakfast," Francine explained, once again giving her nose a swipe.

"She doesn't?"

Sylvia shook her head. "Nope. Too fat."

"She's not fat."

"You know that, and I know that. But remember how you guys always tease her at school? 'Wall Street the Walrus,' isn't that what you call her?"

"But that's just a joke. We always tease you girls about being fat."

"Which is why we're always dieting."

"That stinks," I cried.

"Tell me about it," Sylvia said.

"But I'm starving!"

"We all are, Wally."

Francine pushed up her glasses, gave a couple

more sniffs for good measure, and looked to her watch. "We better get a move on, Wallace. The day *sniff* is young, and we've barely begun."

Chapter 3

Something in the Air

I headed down the school hallway with Francine on one side and Sylvia on the other. A couple of dozen guys, and at least that many girls, surrounded us.

"Give up, McDoogle," the female types shouted. "There's no way you're good enough to be a girl."

"Come on, McDoogle," the guys shouted. "Be a real man and be a woman."

And then, passing the other direction in the hall, I saw the same size crowd surrounding Wall Street. At least I thought it was Wall Street. It was pretty hard to tell under all the grime, dirty clothes, and matted hair.

"Wall Street," I shouted. "Wall Street, is that you?"

She looked up. There was no missing the pain in her eyes.

"This is terrible," she called. "They only let me in the bathroom for nineteen seconds this morning. Then they made me eat so much breakfast I'm about ready to explode."

"It's just the opposite with me," I cried.

"Listen," she asked, "I'm heading off to English. This switching places doesn't count for our schoolwork, does it? I mean I can try and get an A on my English quiz, right?"

"No way." One of Wall Street's officials stepped forward. He was an obvious friend of Bruce Breakaface. I could tell by his similar abuse of the English language. "Real men, we ain't supposed to, uh, be good at, uh . . . uh. . . ."

"English," somebody whispered.

"Yeah, uh . . . at English and stuff like that there kinda stuff."

"That's not true," I argued. "I do great in English."

"I know, but I'm talkin' like real men."

I looked at his body then down at mine. "I think I *gots* your point," I mumbled in agreement.

"Besides, Mc*Fool*gel," Sylvia jabbed her finger at me, "the same goes with you and science. For the next three days, you have to fail all your math and science quizzes."

"But that's no fair," Wall Street protested. "I do great in math and science."

"Sorry," Sylvia shrugged, "but if we're going for stereotypes here, we've got to go all the way. Girls aren't supposed to be good at science, and boys aren't supposed to be good at English."

"That's so stupid," Wall Street cried.

"And it's so wrong," I added.

Sylvia shrugged. "Those are the rules."

Suddenly Francine's hand shot up from the crowd. (I could tell it was her hand by the glistening nose sheen on the back of it.) "Wallace, *sniff* Wallace, we forgot *sniff-sniff* something."

Before I could stop her, she moved toward me and sprinkled a drop or two of perfume over my head. Well, it was supposed to be a drop or two. But when I put out my arm to stop her, I hit the bottle and the whole thing spilled onto me.

Immediately, I could feel my nose begin to itch and tickle.

"Oh no," I cried. "I'm aller . . . aller . . . aller-CHOO . . . to perfume."

"No kidding *sniff ,*" Francine beamed. "So *sniff* am I!"

"Is that why you're always sniff . . . sniff . . . sniffCHOOing?" I asked.

"That's *sniff* right. *sniff.*"

But before we could talk anymore, or at least open up a chapter of Hay Fever's Anonymous, another voice barged in.

"McDoogle . . . Hey, McDoogle." It was good ol' Brucey Baby in all of his menacing dread. "We gots to talk."

"What a . . . abou . . . abCHOO?" I asked, sneezing directly into his face.

He glared at me. But whatever was on his mind was more important than rearranging my facial features. "Da football teams gots play-offs tomorrow night."

"So?"

"So if you ain't there with us like you always is, we're in trouble."

"But I never . . . ever . . . ev—" I put my finger under my nose and managed to hold back the sneeze. "I never play."

"I knows that. But you're like our psychological advantage. Da other team looks across at you and figures if we lets wimpos like you on da bench, we must be hurtin'. Then we surprise 'em and clobber 'em to pieces."

"So . . . oo . . . oo," again my finger went under my nose.

"So you gots ta puts dis babe away a day early so you cans be wit us."

"I don't . . . on't—" more fingers under the nose. "I don't know."

"Oh I does, McDoogle." He drug me up to his face until we were an inch apart. "The ways I sees it, you're either gonna be sittin' on dat bench victorious and alive . . . or defeated and dead. But you are gonna be on dat bench. Gots it?"

I nodded quickly. "Yes, I got . . . got . . . got-CHOO!"

Unfortunately I'd run out of fingers.

Bruce stood there a moment, holding me, blinking, and looking like someone just caught in a very heavy rainstorm. Then, just before he went into action, just before he gave me a lifetime's gift of free dental work, the bell rang and my worries were over.

Well, not exactly . . .

"Hey, McDorkoid," Sylvia demanded, "what's your first class?"

I looked at her and answered. "P.E."

For the very first time all morning I saw Sylvia Wisenmouth break into a smile. It was then I knew I was in real trouble.

* * * * *

I suppose some guys would think it's cool to hang out with the girls' P.E. class. You know, they want to show off their muscles, let the babes see what big, tough athletes are really made of. Unfortunately I'm not such a hot athlete . . . although I did try out for the gum-chewing team last semester and almost made it—except for the part where I had to walk and chew at the same time.

It's not that I don't have coordination. It's just that I've always understood the letters P.E. to stand for Physical Embarrassment.

Today was no different. Mrs. Rumpster, the P.E. teacher, had us outside practicing our archery. Well, the girls were outside practicing their archery. I was just trying to get the arrows the right direction in the bow. (Hey, it's not my fault they don't come with instructions.)

"Uh, no, Wallace," Mrs. Rumpster said. "You hold the feather end in your hands and face the pointy part toward the target."

"Oh, right," I lied, "I knew that."

I quickly flipped the arrow around, placed it against the string, and pulled back on the bow.

"Uh, Wallace—"

"I've got it," I said.

"Well, actually, you may wish to—"

"No, I've got it, I've got it." With great care I took aim at the target, pulled back farther, and let her rip.

It was beautiful the way the bow sailed through the air, the way it almost reached the target, the way the rest of the class threw themselves down on the ground and laughed hysterically.

"Normally, it's the arrow you want to shoot," Mrs. Rumpster explained, "not the bow."

"What?"

"The idea is to let go of the arrow, not the bow."

I looked at the arrow still in my hand. So, I'm like supposed to know everything?

After a couple more minutes of uncontrollable laughter the class finally got a grip on itself, and I was allowed to continue my public display of humiliation. Of course it took a few more sailing bows and a half-dozen broken arrows before I finally got the hang of it. But soon I was firing those beauties through the air like there was no tomorrow.

True, I was having a little problem with aim. And I felt bad about the four windows I busted out over at the school, and the three tires I'd shish-kebabed over in the teachers' parking lot. Then, of course, there were those five kids who had to be taken to the hospital. But you really couldn't blame me. I mean, I wasn't the one who gave me all those sharp pointy objects. It's not my fault they hadn't read any of my books. Otherwise they'd have known I can barely use a toothpick without stabbing myself to death.

Still, I did feel kinda bad. But not as bad as when I saw Ms. Finglestooper running out to me waving a paper in her hand.

"Wally," she cried, "Wally, I've got great news!"

"Get down, Ms. Finglestooper!" Mrs. Rumpster cried. "He's still got one arrow left in his hand!"

But Ms. Finglestooper was a courageous woman who knew no fear, or maybe she knew no intelligence. Because, unlike the rest of the class, who were still huddled on the ground with their heads covered and whimpering for mercy, Ms. Finglestooper continued straight toward me.

"Wally! Wally, I've got great news about your competition with Wall Street!"

"Is it over?" I asked hopefully.

"Not at all. I just got a call from one of the TV networks. They heard what you're trying to prove, and they're sending out a video crew!"

"What?" I asked in astonishment. It was bad enough that the bet between Wall Street and me had become known around the school . . . but now . . . now they were putting us on TV!

"Which network?" I asked. "Which show?"

"That's the beauty of it," Ms. Finglestooper cried. "It's not just one network. It's every network. They're all sending out crews, they all want the story. This little bet of yours is going to be broadcast coast-to-coast!"

Chapter 4

Pass the Cookies . . . to Someone Else

By the time Home Economics rolled around, I was feeling a bit stressed. But skipping breakfast, being baptized in perfume, and doing a pretty bad imitation of Robin Hood on the archery range wasn't quite enough. Now it was time to continue the torture with sewing lessons.

"Now class," Mrs. Permagrin said in all of her perpetual cheeriness, "just insert the needle into the back of the cloth and shove it through to the front."

(I'll save you the gory details and just remind you how skilled I was with pointy objects in the last chapter.)

After going to the nurse's office and receiving a blood transfusion, I returned to class only to discover that everybody was now baking. Cool. I could handle that. Just do everything my little sister Carrie doesn't when she cooks. No problem.

Well . . . except for the part where they'd just run out of baking powder.

"What do I need baking powder for?" I asked.

"It gives it a little extra kick." Mrs. Permagrin smiled. "And it helps the cookies to rise."

I grinned. "I've got the perfect solution. I'll be right back."

After a little searching, I found the solution over in the science class. It was a small canister of gunpowder. I knew it wouldn't taste the same, but if baking powder gave the dough a "little extra kick," then gunpowder ought to really help it out.

I headed back to class feeling pretty smug and knowing that I was really going to impress the class.

When I entered the room Mrs. Permagrin was still smiling as she shot a fire extinguisher at someone's pan of burning cookies. "Nothing to worry about, dear." She grinned as she spoke to the crying girl. "Some people actually like their cookies well done."

I headed to my counter, opened the canister, and dumped just a dash of the secret powder into my dough. It was black, which gave the dough an odd look, but I figured it was okay. Then I figured something else. If a little powder is good, then a lot ought to be better. I poured in more, mixed it up, and dropped the delectable little dough globs onto a greased pan. Ten minutes later I pulled them out of the oven. Incredibly, they looked and smelled exactly like . . . well, exactly like cookies. (And you thought something bad was going to happen, didn't you? Come on, admit it.) But to my surprise (and yours), it didn't.

I scooped the cookies off the pan and set them in one long perfect row on the counter.

I was so impressed with myself that I quickly made up another batch and threw them in the oven just as Mrs. Permagrin passed by.

"Oh, Wallace." She smiled her perpetual smile. "They're so beautiful."

"Thanks," I said, feeling more than a little proud.

She leaned over them for a closer look. "Tell me, what is this black color from?"

"Oh, that," I hedged, while I carefully tried to hide the can of gunpowder behind me on the counter. I almost succeeded—except for the part where I bumped into the stove and accidentally turned on one of the gas burners.

Even that wouldn't have been so bad if the first cookie hadn't been so close to the flame.

K-BAMB!

The thing exploded like a firecracker, right on the counter. Everyone, including Mrs. Permagrin, jumped back and screamed.

Apparently, I'd put a little too much 'kick' into the cookie dough. Worse yet, that explosion was only the beginning. Because that cookie was touching the next cookie

K-BAMB! K-BAMB!

which was touching the next

K-BAMB! K-BAMB! K-BAMB!

By now everyone was screaming and racing for the door. For a moment even Mrs. Permagrin's smile seemed to falter as she dashed out of the room.

K-BAMB! K-BAMB! K-BAMB! K-BAMB!

I was the last to leave. (I would have been the first if I hadn't wasted all that time screaming in panic, running into other kids, and falling over chairs.) But, as I arrived at the door, I kept thinking I was forgetting something. It was then that I looked back to the counter.

I wished I hadn't.

Because there, sitting at the very end of the row of cookies, was the canister of gunpowder.

K-BAMB! K-BAMB! K-BAMB!
K-BAMB! K-BAMB!

The cookies were acting like a long fuse, working their way down to the gunpowder. I started to pray, begging God not to send me to where all bad cooks go (the last thing I wanted to do was eat my sister's cooking for eternity), when finally, it happened

KA - B O O M ! ! ! !

* * * * *

I woke up on a stretcher beside the ambulance. A paramedic was hovering over me, and about a hundred TV cameras were shoved in my face. All the big-time reporters were there . . . Dan Rathernot, Tom Brokenoff, even that old-timer, Walter Crankcase. It seems everyone was pushing a microphone into my face and asking questions.

"Do you still think girls have it easier than boys?"

"Are you still continuing the competition?"

"Did you really try to blow up the school because you were afraid of losing?"

It was then I noticed the smoldering remains of the Home Economics classroom behind them and the half-dozen or so fire trucks. I was about to explain that it was just another McDoogle mishap and nothing to worry about, when Barbara Warters cried, "There she is! There's Wall Street!"

Suddenly the whole herd turned and chased after Wall Street. I started to get up, but the paramedic pushed me back down.

"Lay back and rest," he ordered.

"But—"

"Everything's okay, you just need to take it easy."

I nodded and lay back down. That's when I spotted Ol' Betsy by my side. With nothing else to do (except wonder how much worse things could get) I decided to check up on Bumble Boy. Compared to the insanity surrounding me, a nice, amped-out, action-packed, nail-biting story should help me relax.

When we last left Bumble Boy, he was dashing out of the hive to battle the sickeningly sinister and shamefully showy Shakespeare Guy. Already this artistically challenged archenemy is making people sound like Macbeth, Hamlet, or any of those other weird guys carrying around skulls and talking funny.

But it isn't just their words. As Bumble Boy buzzes toward New York City he sees an army troop trading in its rifles for fencing swords, gang members replacing their baggy pants with black tights, and construction workers chucking their hard hats for feathered caps.

It's terrible. No, it's worse than terrible. It's like having your TV permanently stuck on an educational channel!

But that's only the beginning. Suddenly, there's a high-pitched scream overhead. It sounds like a large, flying bat. Our superhero lifts his superhero head and with his keen superhero vision detects that—gasp of gasps...it's a large flying bat. (Hey, he didn't graduate from Superhero U without learning something.)

Unfortunately the bat is now diving directly for him. Now, Bumble Boy likes to be the center of attention as much as the next guy. In fact, he was even hoping to sign an autograph for the

creature and maybe pose for a photo
with him. But the way the thing is diving toward him and opening its mouth,
he realizes the bat isn't interested in
a free autograph...he wants a free
lunch!

I know, I know. One of you bright types
is asking if bats really eat bumble bees
with stingers. (Probably the same kid who
had the exoskeleton question earlier.)
How should I know? Maybe they eat everything but the stinger and save that for
last, like a toothpick or something. Who
knows? Certainly not Bumble Boy. And
since he doesn't have time to check it
out on the Internet, and since he's
allergic to being eaten by bats (he
breaks out in a bad case of death every
time it happens), Bumble Boy does what
any superhero in his right mind with
wings would do. He flies for his life!

He drops down and begins buzzing
through trees, swooping in and out of
the branches.

It does no good. Bat boy is right
behind him.

He drops lower, darting through the
flowers, this way and that—that way and

this. But the creature stays on his tail as close as those bad guys in the Star Wars movies (but without all the cool sound effects).

Desperately, our hero looks for a place to hide. Somewhere nice and dark, since he figures bats can't see in the dark. (Hey, just because he has a superbody doesn't mean he has a superbrain.)

He spots a nearby cave, darts inside, and breathes a sigh of relief. There's no way the bat will get to Bumble Boy now. Not when he has to fight over him with all the other 50,000 bats.

ALL THE OTHER 50,000 BATS!

That's right. As we've previously established, ol' Bumble Brain will not be winning any genius contests. Apparently, he chose a giant cave full of bats to hide in. This is no problem if you like flying around in the dark and happen to enjoy eating insects. But it's a big problem if you can't see in the dark and happen to be an insect.

Suddenly, Bumble Boy is the life of the party. Literally.

Everyone wants a piece of him. In fact, everyone is going batty over him. (Come on, you knew I'd work that one in.) Of course he tries some lame lie, like saying he thought it was a costume party and he came disguised as a bumble bee. But nobody swallows it.

However, somebody does swallow him.

One minute he's in pitch blackness surrounded by thousands of wings, the next minute he's in pitch blackness surrounded by some very large bat tonsils.

But realizing he cannot die this early in the story, our hero decides to do a little poking around. Literally. He begins his world famous dentist routine and, using his stinger, jabs the creature deep in its gums. It lets out a loud, angry cry

SQUEAK! SQUEAK! SQUEAK!

As the bat opens its mouth, Bumble Boy sees an escape route and makes a "bee-line" (come on, you knew that was coming, too) out of the cave.

Unfortunately

HONK...HONK...

Oh no, he's flying too close to the freeway. A giant tanker truck is barreling down on him. Any moment he's going to wind up being bug splat on some grill. Then—just as he wonders what the last thing to go through his mind will be (and hoping it's not going to be his stinger)—the truck catches his left set of legs and sends him tumbling out of control, antenna over heels, until

Whop Whop Whop Whop Whop Whop . . .

I looked up from my computer and saw a giant helicopter dropping over our heads and landing in the parking lot.

People were rushing around every which way . . . including Ms. Finglestooper.

"What's going on?" I shouted.

"It's the Governor," she cried in excitement.

"The Governor?"

"That's right. She's running for president, and she thinks your bet with Wall Street is the perfect campaign issue."

"The what?"

"She's going to use you as an example of how all men are male chauvinistic slobs and how they are actually inferior to women."

"She's what?"

"Isn't this exciting?" she shouted. "You'll stand for what's wrong with all the men in our country. You'll debate her on national TV. You'll get to be publicly humiliated by one of the most powerful women in the world!"

I glanced down at my superhero story and let out a long sigh. Needless to say, I was pretty envious of Bumble Boy. Being a permanent hood ornament on a tanker truck sounded a whole lot better than my current fate.

"Come on, Wallace," Ms. Finglestooper cried, motioning for me to follow. "Come on, the whole world is waiting."

Chapter 5

Political Correctness

"Where is he?" Governor Makeasplash cried, as she stepped off the helicopter. She began scanning the crowd. "Where is that woman-hating, sexist, Wally McBigot?"

The good news was there were a zillion and one people in the crowd. I figured I could just sort of blend in. The bad news was all zillion (except this one) took three steps back, leaving me out in the open. Now she could clearly see me. I was all alone like a deer trapped in the glaring headlights of this woman's political ambition. (Wow, what a phrase; I should be a writer or something.)

She stormed from the helicopter and headed directly for me. I was history, dead meat, just so much plaque on the dental floss of life. (Wow, there's another one.) But before I could collect my Pulitzer Prize for such incredible writing, she had arrived. Talk about mad. She looked like she wanted to bite off my head. But when she saw the camera lights come on she suddenly turned all smiles.

"Well, hello there, Wallace," she said, extending her hand.

For a second I hesitated. But I realized I had an extra arm—in case she thought of ripping the first off and beating me over the head with it. So, I agreed to shake her hand.

A thousand flashbulbs went off.

"It's so nice to meet you," she said, still grinning. "What a privilege to speak with a young man unafraid to state his opinions." Her act was so convincing that I forgot about my Pulitzer Prize and wondered when she'd be picking up her Oscar.

"You're—you're not mad?" I stuttered.

"Mad," she forced a chuckle, then turned so all the cameras could see her. More flashes. "Mad?" she repeated, in case anybody missed a flash. "Of course I'm not mad."

I breathed a sigh of relief. "Good, because I really didn't—"

She interrupted. "No, my good boy, I'm not mad at all."

"Good, 'cause I think there was a mix-up, because I never really—"

"After all, it's not your fault that your thinking is the product of our country's bias and sexist mentality."

"Well, actually, I think—"

"It's not your fault that you think men are superior to women."

"Actually, I believe—"

"It's not your fault that you and your generation are merely the natural extension of the current administration's outdated and antiquated policies painfully manifesting the . . ."

I'm not sure when she quit talking English, but suddenly she was making no sense. In fact, with all the cameras and reporters surrounding her, I got the feeling she wasn't even talking to me.

". . . a clear and persuasive illustration of the administration's lack of sensitivity regarding gender. . . ."

See what I mean?

And then it dawned on me. If she wasn't talking to me, maybe she wouldn't miss me. And if she wouldn't miss me, maybe I could just sort of slip away—unnoticed. It was worth a try. As she continued talking her political pig Latin, I slowly eased myself over to the edge of the crowd.

So far so good.

". . . were I to begin my tenure in the executive office I guarantee you I would immediately institute legislation assuring the rights of . . ."

I slowly slipped into the crowd.

So far, so good.

I kept looking at the Governor, pretending I was

listening, while slowly walking backwards . . . ten, fifteen, twenty feet. I tell you it was a work of art, the way I was making my getaway. Like poetry in mot—

"Ow! Watch it!"

I spun around and saw . . .

"Wall Street!" I cried in a whisper.

"Wally!" she whispered back, equally surprised. She looked very tired and beat up. In fact, she looked almost as bad as I felt.

"What happened to you?" I asked.

"The usual guy stuff," she shrugged. "Wedgies by the bullies in the hallway, swirlies by the jocks in the lavatories. And automotive shop. How was I supposed to know you couldn't arc weld a gas can when it's full of gas? I almost blew up the place."

I threw a look over to the smoking remains of the Home Economics building. It seemed like we were having equally bad days.

"I tell you, Wally," she shook her head. "You're right, I'm just not cut out for all this guy stuff."

"I'm not as right as you are," I said. "Doing all this girl stuff is killing me."

She let out a long, low sigh. "And now I've got to go to your football practice."

"And I have to go to your ballet rehearsal."

"Maybe . . ." her eyes started to brighten in hope. "Maybe we should just call the whole thing off."

Of course, what a brilliant solution! I began to nod. "Yes! We can admit that we were both wrong and that—"

"There they are!" someone shouted.

I spun around.

The whole crowd of reporters turned their attention and cameras back on us. They swarmed around us like sharks circling raw meat.

"So tell us, Wall Street," they said as they shoved mics in front of her face. "How are you handling this competition? Are you about ready to give up?"

"I don't know," she sighed. "Maybe. Wally and I were just talking, and maybe it's time—"

"Are you admitting defeat?" one of the reporters shouted. "Are you agreeing that boys are superior to girls?"

"I didn't say that," she corrected. "I don't believe boys are superior, but—"

"Did you hear that, Wally?" another reporter shouted. "She doesn't believe you guys are superior? Are you going to let her get away with that?"

"Well, no. I mean yes," I stammered. "I mean of course not."

"So you believe that girls are inferior?"

"In some things. . . . Yeah, I suppose, but in other things—"

"Did you hear that?" they spun back to Wall Street. "Are you going to take that? Are you really going to give up and admit boys are better?"

"No way," Wall Street said. "Boys are not better."

"You hear that, Wally?" another reporter cried. "She says girls are the superior ones."

I don't know what happened. Suddenly our words were getting all twisted around. I couldn't figure out why Wall Street was saying all those things when just minutes ago she and I had agreed.

"So are you licked, Wally?" another reporter shouted.

I could feel myself getting angry.

"Are you defeated? Is that what you're saying?" they shouted. "Do you agree with her that girls are the superior ones!"

I finally exploded. "Only in her dreams!" I shouted.

"Oh yeah?" Wall Street said, stepping toward me. I could tell she was as mad as I was.

"Yeah." I said, refusing to back down. "It's way harder being a guy than a girl."

"Is not."

"Is too."

"Is not."

"Is too."

She got into my face. "Is not."

I got into hers. "Is too."

Somewhere in the back of my mind this was all sounding very familiar. Too familiar. But before I could figure it out, our beloved Governor pushed her way through the crowd. After all, she'd been out of the spotlight for almost a minute, and it was obvious she was going through some sort of attention withdrawal.

"Children, children," she clapped her hands, once again becoming all poise and grace. "I see we still have ourselves a dilemma, don't we?"

We said nothing.

She cranked up her smile a couple of notches above phony. "Well, there really is only one solution, isn't there?"

Wall Street and I turned to the Governor, waiting for the answer. She rested one hand on my shoulder and one on Wall Street's. "You must continue the competition. And you have my promise that these folks from the press and I will not leave your sides until we see a victor."

Wall Street glared into my eyes. "That's fine with me," she growled.

I glared right back. "Make mine a double fine."

"Excellent," the Governor chuckled, "excellent."

I knew things weren't going exactly as we'd planned, but before I could sort through the details, I felt a hand grab my arm.

"All right, McDorkel. . . ." It was my part-time referee and full-time pain in the neck, Sylvia Wisenmouth. She started pulling me through the crowd.

"Where are we going?" I demanded.

"You're late for ballet rehearsal."

"But I was talking to the Governor."

"Oh, she'll be seeing you again, McDumbo. Didn't you just hear? The Governor, the press, everyone will be watching you. Yes sir, the entire world is going to be watching every move you make."

"Wonderful," I sighed, "what else can go wrong?" Unfortunately I was about to get my answer.

Chapter 6

A Smokin' Rehearsal

"Come out, McDimwit," Sylvia Wisenmouth called from the other side of the door. "They're waiting to begin rehearsal."

"No way," I shouted. "Not in these clothes." I looked down. Over my T-shirt and gym shorts I had on a ridiculous looking pink tutu and ballet slippers. Not exactly the type of clothes I'd want to be seen alive in. Come to think of it, I wouldn't want to be seen dead in them either.

"But it's dress rehearsal." Francine sniffed from the other side of the door. "That was Wall Street's costume as the Sugar Plum Fairy, and now it has to be yours."

"Forget it."

"So are you forfeiting?" Sylvia called. "Should I tell Bruce Breakaface and the guys that you've finally given up, that you agree girls are tougher than boys?"

Ah, good ol' Bruce. I'd almost forgotten. To die or not to die, that is the question. Is it better to give up one's pride and thus keep one's life, or to give up one's life and thus— I shook my head; it was definitely time to cut back on writing that Shakespeare Guy story.

"Come on, Wally."

Like it or not, I knew I had to come out. Besides, it wasn't like it would be a full-blown performance. It was only a dress rehearsal. Only the cast and crew would see me.

So with that comforting thought I reached for the door, pushed it open, and was met by the glaring light of every news reporter and cameraman in the English-speaking world.

I was grateful they didn't ask questions. I guess it's hard to ask questions when you're falling on the ground in fits of uncontrollable laughter. Before they stopped laughing some old woman grabbed me by the arm and dragged me down the hall to a large room filled with mirrors.

"Don't you vorry about zem, Master McDoogle."

Her voice sounded familiar, but I couldn't place it. She closed the door behind us and led me to a long ballet barre about waist high. "Before ve begin ze rehearsal ve vill vork on your vlexibility."

Where had I heard that voice? Where had . . .

"Virst ve do zee stretching exerzizes."

Suddenly I had it!

"Ve put your right leg up on ze bar like zo."

It was Ms. Stanaslobsky, the Russian ballet teacher way back from *My Life As a Human Hockey Puck!* The very one who tried to stretch me into a Gumby doll!

"No," I cried, "I don't stretch. Remember, I'm the one who—"

Before I could finish she'd lifted my leg to the bar and pushed down on my shoulders.

"And den ve push you down like zo—"

It was just like old times; same pain, same screaming, and of course the same

RIPPPPPing

of every muscle in my leg. It was everything I remembered and more.

"Zo," she said when we were finally through. "Now don't you veel better all limbered up?"

I nodded my head like a lunatic. (If I didn't, I knew she'd keep stretching me until I either died or became too tall to play for the Chicago Bulls.)

"Un now ve begin ze rehearsal."

The good news was she kept the press out of the auditorium while the cast and I rehearsed the dance. The bad news was I didn't know the first thing about dancing.

"Don't vorry about dat, Master McDoogle," Ms. Stanaslobsky kept saying. "Jus veel ze muzic. Become von vis ze muzic."

She nodded to the orchestra, and they began to play. All the other dancers dashed out onto the stage. They began leaping and dancing around a giant rock with an old-fashioned kerosene lantern burning on top of it. It was really kind of pretty with the lantern and the costumed dancers. And directly behind them were giant walls of scenery painted to look exactly like a snowy forest. There was only thing missing.

"Vere is our Sugar Plum Fairy?" Ms. Stanaslobsky called. "Vere is our Sugar Plum Fairy?"

I could tell by the way all eyes shot to me that I was the missing dancer. I poked my head onto the stage and looked out to Ms. Stanaslobsky.

"Don't vorry, Master McDoogle," she called from the audience. "All you need to do is veel ze muzic. Jus become von vis ze muzic and veel it."

Now it's true, I'd never danced in my life, but I'd seen them do it on TV lots of times. It didn't look too tough. Besides, if all I had to do was "veel ze muzic," I could probably handle that. So, with a deep breath, I stepped out on the stage and started running around the rock with all the other dancers.

"Very good, Master McDoogle. Veel it. Become von vis ze muzic and jus veel it."

I did everything she said, and, sure enough, pretty soon I started getting into it. Who cared if I didn't know how to dance or if I didn't know any of the steps? The point is I was really "veeling it." It wasn't my fault that the other dancers kept turning and stopping without bothering to signal. And you really couldn't blame me for knocking most of them to the ground before the end of the first song.

Still, I must have been pretty good because the ones still standing couldn't wait to dash off the stage and watch my moves from the safety of the wings. I could tell they were impressed by the way they kept shaking their heads and dropping their mouths open in astonishment.

Since everyone was looking at me, and since I was still "veeling ze muzic", I decided to give them a little treat and show them some real talent.

The music had started again, so I picked up my pace and began to twirl with it. Around and around I went, faster and faster . . . and still faster. Then I changed direction. Unfortunately my head and stomach were still kind of partial to the first direction. Suddenly I felt sick in a major "lose-my-cookies" sort of way. I tried covering my mouth and running straight toward the restroom, but it's hard running straight toward anything when you've been spinning like a top.

The good news was I didn't throw up on anybody or fall off the stage and break any major body parts.

But there was some bad news. Like my gently bumping into one of the towering walls of scenery. Well, "gently bumping" may not be the right phrase. It was more like plowing into the thing with all of my might. I knocked it from its supports, and we all watched as it teetered back and forth. Until finally, like a giant tree

TIMBER!

it tilted too far and fell over.

Fortunately it didn't fall onto the stage and smash the rock with the kerosene lantern. Unfortunately it fell into the giant wall of scenery beside it—which fell into the wall beside it . . . which fell into the . . . (Well, I'm sure you get the picture.) Like a huge set of dominoes each wall knocked over the next until what had once been a beautiful winter wonderland now looked like a ravaged war zone.

However, we weren't quite done. (After all, we are talking a McDoogle catastrophe, right?) Remember that kerosene lantern that the first wall of scenery had missed? Well, the last wall of scenery didn't. It fell forward, smashing into the rock and shattering the lantern . . . the lantern with all that burning kerosene . . . the burning kerosene that was now spreading all over the floor . . . the floor that was now completely engulfed in flames.

It was all very impressive and rated at least a 12 on the McDoogle Mishap scale of 1–10.

Of course I felt terrible, but it wasn't my fault. If they'd read even one of these books they would have known better. I mean, put me near the chance of any catastrophe happening . . . and it will. It's a law of the universe, like gravity, or centrifugal force, or knowing you'll have to stop the car every 14.3 minutes if your little sister drinks a lot of water before a trip.

Still, rehearsal wasn't a total loss. I mean it was great to see my old friends from the fire department as they hosed down the stage. It had been hours since we'd met back at the Home Economics Department, and it was good to get back together and talk over old times.

Unfortunately there was Ms. Stanaslobsky. I don't want to say she took it badly, but as they carried her out on the stretcher she kept rolling her head back and forth mumbling, "Veel ze muzic, jus veel ze muzic." The poor lady was obviously delirious. Until she saw me. Then her eyes widened in recognition, and she started screaming, "Keep him away from me! Keep him away!"

I smiled sadly. It was nice to see she was getting back in touch with reality.

* * * * *

KNOCK, KNOCK, KNOCK.

"What are we doing here?" I asked Sylvia. We were standing outside on the porch of a stranger's house. "It's seven o'clock at night. I should be home by now."

"Not yet, McBrainless."

Sylvia reached over and rapped on the door again.

KNOCK, KNOCK, KNOCK.

"Whose place is this, anyway?" I demanded. "Why are we here?"

"This is the Frankensterns. Wall Street baby-sits here every Thursday."

"Baby-sits!" I cried. "I don't know the first thing about—"

Just then the front door opened and there stood Francine, the human allergy machine. At least I thought it was Francine. It was kinda hard to tell with all the pillows being bashed over her head and all the kids climbing on top of her.

"You are *sniff* several minutes tardy!" she shouted over the screaming babies and blaring TV.

"Sorry," Sylvia yelled, "Wally gave a special performance at the theater!"

"I hope it was satisfactory," Francine sniffed then ducked just in time to dodge a flying Barbie minivan.

"Let's just say the place was cooking!" Sylvia shouted.

"Well, come in!" Francine yelled, as she opened the door.

Reluctantly, I stepped inside. Now, I don't want to say the kids were tearing up the place, but the living room was definitely untidy in a major nuclear holocaust kind of way. Two kids were practicing their mountain climbing on Francine, another was using a felt pen to connect all the flowers on the living room wallpaper, another was playing 'barber' with the family poodle. (Or was it a pet rat? At this stage it was pretty hard to tell.) Then, of course, there were the usual pillow fights (complete with split pillow cases and flying feathers) and a baby screaming her head off.

"How many kids do they have?" I shouted.

"Six or *sniff* seven. It's hard to—DUCK!"

We all ducked just in time to avoid a flying six-year-old who had launched himself through the air by using a nearby ceiling fan.

"They haven't eaten yet," Francine shouted as we climbed back to our feet, "but all the directions are on the kitchen counter!" She quickly headed toward the door.

Sylvia followed. "We'll be by to pick you up at ten!" she yelled over her shoulder.

"Ten o'clock?" I cried. "That's three hours! You're not going to leave me here all alone for three hours!"

Sylvia turned back to me. "Alone?"

I nodded, lost in helplessness.

"No way, we're not leaving you alone."

I breathed a sigh of relief.

"You'll have all six of these cuties to keep you company," she snickered.

"Or seven," Francine corrected.

They were halfway out the door and shutting it when I shouted, "Wait a minute! You can't just leave me here. I don't know how to baby-sit. I mean, what if I do something wrong? What if I accidentally injure them or something?"

Sylvia turned back to me one last time. "*You* injure *them?*"

I nodded yes desperately.

"I'm afraid you've got it all wrong, McDorkel. If there's anybody going to be injured in this house, it ain't going to be the kids." With that she shut the door (not, of course, without a chilling, sinister laugh).

Slowly I turned back to face the room. All six pairs of eyes (or was it seven?) locked onto me—each and every one of the little creatures waiting to see what I would do.

"Uh . . . Hi there," I said giving them a nervous little wave.

They said nothing, but started creeping toward me—the drooling babies crawling, the teething toddlers toddling, and the older ones circling around behind with everything from GI Joe bazookas to toy stun guns (at least I hoped they were toys).

I took a deep breath (though the condition of somebody's diaper made me wish I hadn't). I couldn't back down. It was time to take charge, time to show them what I was really made of, time to race for the bathroom as fast as I could and lock myself inside before they got me.

That was the plan. Unfortunately not every one of my plans comes off exactly the way I'd like.

Chapter 7

Under Attack

KNOCK, KNOCK, KNOCK.

It was just like old times. Somebody was pounding on my door waiting for me to come out.

KNOCK, KNOCK, KNOCK.

Unfortunately those somebodies weren't my good buddies Sylvia and Francine. They were the monster buddies I was expected to baby-sit.

"Pwease come out, Mister McDoogle," they called from the other side of the bathroom door. "Pwease, we pwomise not to hurt you." Call me a skeptic, but somehow I had my doubts.

"Pwease, Mister McDoogle, we're awfully hungwy. We pwomise not to hurt you if you make us some dinna. Pwease, pwetty pwease. . . ."

It was about this time that I noticed the three

inches of water I was standing in—the three inches of water that was quickly rising to four, then five, then . . . I glanced over to the toilet. Someone had tried to flush an Imperial Star Fighter down it. Now everything was stopped up . . . well, except for the water that kept spilling onto the floor and rising around my ankles.

"Pwease, Mister McDoogle. Pwetty pwease."

I was trapped. I could either stay in there and practice my backstroke or go out and face the monsters. And since I didn't have a backstroke (much less a front stroke), I knew I had only one choice.

"Okay, guys," I shouted. "Listen up. If I come out, do you promise not to do anything mean to me?"

"We pwomise," they all shouted.

"No stun guns, no exploding anythings?"

"Absowutly."

I looked down to the water that was now somewhere around my knees. It was now or never. Preparing for the worst, I reached for the door, unlocked it, and threw it open. There they stood, in all their wide-eyed innocence.

"Pwease, we're so hungwy," they said in their helpless little voices.

Some were even getting their bottom lips to tremble. Yes sir, these guys were good, very good. And if it hadn't been for their torn clothing, as well as the bloodstains on the walls and carpet (not to mention that poor shaved poodle, or was it a rat, that kept running around whimpering), I would have bought their act.

I carefully eased down the hall and into the kitchen as I heard their mischievous little feet pattering behind me. I was encouraged to see the youngest baby playing safely in her playpen. (The fact that the playpen was upside down, putting her in a type of prison, was even more encouraging.)

Knowing I had to get them on my side as soon as possible, I asked if they wanted to help me fix dinner. "Anybody want to be Wally's little helper?"

A thousand grimy little hands shot up, and a thousand little mouths all screamed "I do, I do, I do!"

Great, I already had them wrapped around my little finger. I tell you, this baby-sitting business was a breeze. All you had to do was use a little simple psychology.

We started fixing dinner. Since I was bushed, I did my best to convince them to go for something easy—like a glass of water, or maybe some nice dry toast, or, if worse came to worst, a wonderful bowl of cold cereal (without milk, of course).

Unfortunately the kids were a little more demanding. I'll save you all of the foot stomping, tantrums, and tears (and if you think *I* acted badly, you should have seen *them*). To make a long story short, we went for the standard fare of . . . honey-coated sugar cubes, syrup covered Twinkies, and chocolate-covered radishes. (The radishes were my idea because everybody needs vegetables. Right?)

Everything was going pretty well until we got to the baby's meal.

"Momma always bwends stuff for her in the bwender."

No problem. I grabbed the blender and tossed a bunch of healthy junk into it like carrots, celery, tomatoes, and some peanut butter cups. Although it was my first time using a blender, I handled it like a pro—except for the part about forgetting to put on the lid.

I hit the "high" button, and suddenly the air was filled with flying vegetables. They splattered against the cupboards, the walls, and me.

But that was the good news.

Before I could scrape off the goo from my glasses—so I could find the "off" button—one of the little darlings thought it would be fun to play Bazooka. He hopped up on the counter and started dropping other things into the spinning blender. Things like frozen peas

PING, PING, PING, PING.

We were suddenly pelted with hundreds of frozen, green BBs.

Next came the squeeze bottle of chocolate

FLING, FLING, FLING, FLING.

Suddenly we all looked like my chocolate-covered radishes . . . so did the ceiling, doors, and that poor hairless dog, or whatever it was.

And finally there was the box of uncooked spaghetti

K-THWACK, K-THWACK, K-THWACK
"YEOW!!!!!!!!!!!!"

Suddenly we had hundreds of pieces of hard, uncooked spaghetti sticking out of our skin. That was enough. Everyone had had it with Bazooka Boy. Now looking very much like human porcupines, they decided to fight back.

First it was with a flying cup or two (the fact that they were still full of milk made it a little messier). Then they graduated to flying dishes, (fortunately they were plastic; unfortunately they hurt just as bad), and finally they moved up to dining room furnishings (chairs were the weapons of choice, though they also settled for vases, hanging pictures, or anything else that wasn't tied down).

I wasn't sure what had gone wrong. A moment ago I'd been in such control. Now things were getting out of hand in a major World War III kind of way. Of course, being the designated grownup I knew it was my job to try and stop them.

"Guys! Guys!" I shouted as I stepped between them.

But of course that only meant I was getting it from both sides—pieces of dill pickles and cookies (the extra chewy caramel kind) from the blender side, and small flying appliances from the other.

Bazooka Boy would not be stopped. He quickly hooked up an extension cord and started driving the other darlings into the living room with a new onslaught of ice-cream bars, dog food, and the ever-popular raw liver.

The other kids staged a counterattack with TV remotes, CDs, and CD players! I couldn't be certain, but for a moment I even thought I saw the poodle flying by (poor thing, he really gets around). Then came the table lamps and potted plants. They were just starting to work on the big-screen TV when, suddenly, to my relief, the door opened.

At least I thought it was to my relief. Right then I wasn't so sure because Mr. and Mrs. Frankensterns, the ones responsible for spawning these creatures, stood aghast in the doorway with their mouths open.

Everything grew very silent. Well, except for the steady drip, drip, drip of an ice-cream bar melting from atop the chandelier and the slurping of the hairless poodle (or was it a rat) as it licked ketchup off the baby's face. Other than that, everything was very quiet.

*   *   *   *   *

I'll save you the gory details (not so much from what the Frankensterns did as from what my dad did). The short version is that in less than one hour I was back home, safe and sound in my room, where, if Dad got his way, I'd be grounded until the year 2077.

I tell you, if I'd ever thought girls had it easy, I'd sure changed my mind—at least whatever mind I had left. It's true, they really had to go through some pretty tough stuff. And by the looks of things, so would I . . . at least for one more day. To make matters worse, that one more day would also include the big football game which Bruce Breakaface so strongly recommended I attend. And worse than that worse was my upcoming debut as a prima ballerina in *The Nutcracker*.

Yes sir, on the scale of happiness, things were definitely pushing a minus 17. So I did what I always do when I'm depressed. I reached for Ol' Betsy, snapped her on, and tried to lose myself

in my superhero story. When I last left Bumble
Boy he was about to be hit by a giant tanker truck.
It was nice to know some people were having a
better day than mine.

The tanker truck smashes into Bumble
Boy. He bounces off the grill and tumbles
antenna over heels until he suddenly
strikes the giant truck's windshield. Or
shall we say the giant truck's windshield suddenly strikes him. But instead
of becoming so much bug splat on the
highway of life (Woo, sounds like a new
country western song.), our little bug
guy only has the pollen knocked off him.
But the wind presses him against the
windshield, pinning him harder than
one of those wrestling guys on TV—
although you'll never catch him wearing those weird leotards and screaming
at the camera, "I'm going to rip off
your head and eat it!"
At last the incredibly intelligent
insect turns his head and looks through
the windshield. He gasps an incredibly
intelligent insect gasp. Thanks to some
creative writing from an author whose
name shall go unmentioned (except that

the first name begins with W, ends in Y, and there's an ALL thrown in the middle somewhere). Anyway, thanks to some very creative writing, the driver of the truck is none other than (insert coincidence music here)...Shakespeare Guy!

"Shakespeare Guy," our hero shouts over the roaring wind, "what are you doing?"

"I'm driving this tanker,
To meet thee in yon city.
Where we shall duketh it out,
In a manner most unpretty."

Shakespeare Guy's poetry is as bad as ever. "But why are you driving this tanker?" our hero shouts. "What's inside it?"

"'Tis the last bit of my potion,
To make the world speak thusly.
But 'tis no matter for you,
Since you'll soon become a
    bug Slushie."

With that, the pouting poet trans-porting the potentially powerful poison potion (say that with a mouthful of crackers) reaches down and turns on the truck's windshield wipers.

Bumble Boy looks up just in time to see a giant windshield wiper blade heading directly toward him. Like a falling guillotine it seems to have only one purpose in life—to end his.

Bumble Boy struggles to get free.

The blade falls faster.

Again, he struggles to get free.

The blade falls faster.

And then, just when our hero is about to be wiped off the windshield (not to mention the face of the earth), he uses his last ounce of superbug strength, leaps high enough to clear the falling blade, and lands on top of it.

(Pretty impressive, huh? That's why they pay him the big superhero bucks.)

Now he sits on top of the swishing wiper blade shouting, "Ee-Ha!" like some cowboy riding a bucking bronco. But Shakespeare Guy hates rodeos. He reaches down to the windshield washer and gives it a squirt. The liquid stream hits our beloved hero, and he starts to choke and gag. Then, just when he's coughing and sputtering more than Grandpa's old pickup (or for that matter, more than Grandpa), the slippery detergent causes him to lose his grip.

Bumble Boy flies from the wiper blade. But, thanks to another incredible coincidence——courtesy of this writer——the wind actually whips him into the truck's open window.

Shakespeare Guy cries in panic, "Alack ...Forsooth!" And, of course, the ever popular:

"AUUUUUUUUUGH-th."

Now the two are battling it out in the truck's cab. Shakespeare Guy is trying to play "squash" with our hero, and our hero is realizing that if he fails to stop him, the entire world will probably all start saying "AUUUUGH-th."

It is a fight to the finish until Shakespeare Guy suddenly reaches into the glove compartment and produces a can of bug spray.

"Better droppeth to your kneesth,
And sayeth a prayerth.

'Cause we've just movedth up,
To chemical warfareth."

   Then with a sinister laugh (the type
learned in bad-guy schools everywhere),
the poor excuse for a poet points the
can toward our hero, places his finger
on the button, and...

   "Okay, Wally!" It was Mom calling from down-
stairs. "Time to get to sleep. You've got a big day
tomorrow; you don't want to be tired."
   With a heavy sigh I shut Ol' Betsy down and
turned off the light. Mom was right. The worst
thing in the world is to be half asleep when you're
about to be executed.

Chapter 8

Political Crackedness

The following morning it was the same drill. The same visit by Sylvia and Francine, the same combing of every one of my hairs, the same pressure at school, and at lunchtime the same death threats from my good buddy, Bruce Breakaface.

"Yos better be sittin' on dat bench tonight or yos in big trouble."

"But—but—but," I continued my motorboat imitation as my mind raced for some solution. "If the other team sees Wall Street sitting there, won't that have the same effect? I mean she is just a girl, right?"

"Are you messing wit me?"

Once again he pulled me into our usual talking position—my fearful face one inch from his snarling mouth.

"Dat girl plays a hundred times better den yos."

I nodded. Of course. What was I thinking?

"Wally. Hey, Wally!"

I looked up to see my other best friend, Opera, whose love for classical music is only surpassed by his love for deep fried, salt saturated fat (with a little potato chip hidden in the middle).

"Hey, Opera, what's up?"

"I just *crunch* talked to Wall Street *crunch, crunch*." He was working on his third bag of the day.

"How's she doing?"

"Awful *munch-crunch*. In fact *crunch-munch*, she looks almost as bad as you *burp*. She doesn't know if she can take another day."

I nodded, knowing exactly what she meant.

"And with the football game coming up and the ballet and the President visiting—"

"Woaaa . . . ," I interrupted. "The President?"

He nodded, letting out a loud belch for good measure.

"President of what?" I asked.

"Of the country, Wally. He heard Governor Makeasplash on TV yesterday, and since they're both running for president—"

Before he could finish, we were interrupted by a bunch of shouting, "Stand aside, stand aside!"

I looked up and saw a dozen guys, dressed in suits and wearing little earpieces, pushing through the crowd toward us.

"Step back, please. Give us some room."

Behind them was the usual circus of TV cameras and reporters. Everyone was facing backwards talking to and photographing none other than the President of the United States.

"Are you Willie McDonald?" one of the suits asked me.

I looked to him, then to his earpiece. I'd seen enough movies to know this guy was either an avid baseball fan who couldn't miss a single game, or he was from the Secret Service.

"Yes sir," I said. "Actually it's Wally McDoogle."

"Yeah, right," he said searching the crowd, "whatever."

Suddenly the reporters stepped aside, and there was the President heading directly for me.

"Willard McDurmel?" he asked, arriving and sticking out his hand. "Let me shake your hand."

Nervously I took his hand, and about a thousand cameras started clicking and whirring away.

Without missing a beat, the President turned toward the cameras. "I just want to say, Willard, that you embody the essence of what makes this great republic of ours so great. Think of it, a young man at your tender age and stature willing to endure political lobbyists and special interest groups who assault the time-honored traditions of our forefathers, let alone the proven status quo of . . ."

Suddenly he sounded very much like Governor Makeasplash.

". . . to be cognizant of such an auspicious occasion and as a reminder of my positive impact upon the national deficit . . ."

Same big words, same talking to the cameras and ignoring me.

". . . aware that I will personally be attending your ballet premier this evening thereby offering my moral and political support, a support, I might add, that is indicative of . . ."

Hold it! Did I hear right? Was he going to attend my ballet performance? Was the President of the United States actually going to see me running around in a tutu?

I started to protest but was interrupted by Mrs. Permagrin, from the Home Economics Department (or at least what was left of the Home Economics Department). She was pushing her way through the reporters and calling, "Mr. President, Mr. President. . . ."

She'd no sooner broken through the crowd than every Secret Service man there had his gun out and trained on her.

"It's okay," Ms. Finglestooper cried from the crowd. "She's one of us. She's one of the teachers."

The President nodded, once again becoming all smiles as the Secret Service put away their guns.

Meanwhile, Mrs. Permagrin continued to approach him with a silver tray of cookies. Cookies that looked just like the ones I had made. Cookies with those same odd black specs running through them.

"Mr. President." She grinned as she stepped up to him. "I thought you would enjoy these cookies that Wally baked all by himself."

My mouth dropped open. Where on earth? And then I remembered the second batch I'd put in the oven. When the Home Economics Department was burning down, that second batch of cookies was safe and secure inside the oven.

Seeing the opportunity for a few thousand more photographs, the President laughed. "Why I'd love to try a cookie," he said.

It was like a slow motion movie as the President's hand reached toward the tray of cookies that the grinning Mrs. Permagrin was holding out.

I had to stop them, to warn him. "No," I shouted as I lunged for the tray. "Look out, those cookies are—"

My movement startled Mrs. Permagrin, causing the tray to tilt in her hand, allowing all two dozen of the little cookie bombs to slide off and start hitting the ground

K-BAMB!

K-BAMB! K-BAMB!

Yes sir, it was just like old times . . . except for the Secret Service agents racing at me and tackling me to the ground

"OAFFF!"
K-BAMB! K-BAMB! K-BAMB!

while the other agents were busy throwing their bodies over the President

K-BAMB! K-BAMB!

as the crowd of reporters, teachers, and students began running this way and that, screaming hysterically, "Wally's shot the President! McDoogle's gone mad and has attacked the President!"
See what I mean? Just like old times.

* * * * *

The next few hours were a blur.
First there was my arrest by the Secret Service. Nice guys except for the part of wanting to shoot me first and ask questions later. They were also a little moody. Something about thinking I was trying to kill their boss made them a touch on the cranky side.

In a matter of minutes I found myself hauled into a darkened room, with a spotlight glaring in my face, and the Macarena playing 150 times nonstop in the background. (Boy, do these guys know how to torture somebody, or what?)

I told them the truth about my catastrophe-prone life, but they wouldn't buy it.

"What do you take us for?" Agent One demanded. "Nobody's that much of a dork-oid."

It wasn't until his partner, better known as Agent Two, brought in my file, that they had second thoughts.

"Hmmm . . . ," Agent One said, taking the report and reading it. "Accidentally winding up on the Space Shuttle, turning into a torpedo test target, becoming dinosaur dental floss, reindeer road kill, a bigfoot breath mint." He glanced over to his partner. "Looks like the boy might be telling the truth, after all."

Agent Two shook his head in amazement. "I don't know, kid," he said to me. "That's pretty incredible stuff. You should write it down. Maybe put it into a book someday."

Agent One agreed. "Or a whole series of books."

Then in unison they both shook their heads. "Naw, nobody would believe it."

I glanced at my watch—it was 7:15. The good news was the football game at the school had already started. That meant Brucey Boy would not be dropping by to present me my free, all-expense-paid, face alignment.

The bad news was the agents knew all about my ballet debut and promised to get me there on time. (Suddenly the glaring lights and listening to the Macarena didn't seem so bad.)

Anyway, fifty minutes later I was standing backstage wearing my ballet costume with the pink tutu. I peeked through the curtain at the audience. Everybody was there. Way in the back sat my family, complete with doting sister and snickering brothers. In front of them sat every reporter in the world poised with cameras so they wouldn't miss a thing. Then came Ms. Stanaslobsky, whose medication was cranked up so high, she wouldn't notice a thing, which was probably just as well. In front of her sat Governor Makeasplash and all of her people. And finally, in the very front row sat the President of the United States.

The stagehands had done a great job repairing the stage. Unfortunately, they hadn't quite learned their lesson, because there, high atop the rock, was another burning kerosene lantern.

Uh-oh . . .

The overture was about to start. All of the dancers were getting into place when suddenly a big burly arm grabbed me and pulled me into the wings.

It was the head stagehand. Big, hairy, muscular—kind of like my brothers, but with some sign of intelligence.

"You nervous?" he asked.

I looked up to him and nodded.

He broke into a broad, semi-toothless grin. "Don't be. You're representing all the men from around the world. We ain't about to let you down."

"What do you mean?" I asked.

"We rigged up this here harness." He held out a giant rope with some straps. "Just let me hook this up to you, and I'll be guiding your every move."

"You'll what?"

"If you're gonna run into something, I'll just yank this rope here and pull you out of the way."

I looked at the rope in his hands. It ran all the way up to a pulley attached to a giant beam in the ceiling, and then back down again to form the harness at my end.

He continued. "If you need to do a fancy step, I'm here to help you out. And if you need to jump, I'll give this a tug, and you'll go sailing higher than any girl ever hoped to sail."

I couldn't believe my ears; this was too good to be true. "You'd do that for me?" I croaked.

"Not for you, McDoogle. For men. For all men around the world. It's our duty. We can't let them women win. Now turn around and let me get you strapped into this thing."

For a split second I hesitated. Somewhere in the back of my mind I was wondering if this was really playing fair. But then I thought of Wall Street, our bet, and the idea of finally beating her. That was all it took (that plus the idea of not burning down any more theaters).

I let him tie the harness around me, and he'd barely gotten it hooked up before the music swelled.

"That's your cue, McDoogle. Go, go, go!" He gave me a shove, and I raced onto the stage.

There was a polite round of applause which almost drowned out my father's gasp. (I guess I'd forgotten to tell him about the tutu.)

And then I began to dance.

I tell you, I was incredible. Talk about being light on my feet! All I had to do was nod to the stagehand and he'd pulled the rope and help me do all sorts of impressive moves. The applause grew louder and louder. I could hear the President shouting, "Bravo, bravo." And every time I was about to plow into someone or do serious structural damage to the scenery, the stagehand would simply give me another pull.

I was amazing. As the first song ended and I soared off the stage, the audience was practically on its feet cheering.

"You're doing great, kid!" the stagehand shouted, wiping the sweat from his face. "Let's work in more jumps during this next section and show them what real men can do."

I nodded, catching my breath. And then I heard her. "Wally, Wally."

I spun around to see Wall Street running toward me. She was still in my football uniform, wearing good ol' number 00.

"How'd the game go?" I asked. "Did they cream us?"

"We won." She grinned.

"We won?!" I practically shouted.

She nodded.

"But—how?" I stammered. "How did you do it?"

"Oh, I don't know. Maybe it was because the other side's quarterback couldn't take his eyes off me. Or maybe it was because I just kept batting my baby blues at him. Then of course there was my promise to give him my phone number, but only if we won."

I scowled. Part of me was grateful we'd won (this would definitely cut down on Bruce Breakaface's free dental plan), but part of me was jealous that Wall Street, a girl, had been more helpful to the team than I, a guy.

"What's wrong?" she asked.

"I don't know," I said. "Flirting with the other team, isn't that kinda like cheating?"

"And what about you?" she asked, motioning to the rope and harness. "This isn't exactly playing fair."

Before I could answer, the stagehand hissed, "You're on, McDoogle. You're on!"

I started for the stage. "I don't know about playing fair," I called over my shoulder to Wall Street, "but if you think you were good, check this out."

I headed back onto the stage amidst more applause. Once again I began doing fancy spins, moves, and turns. And once again I could hear the people being wowed. I was even more incredible than the last time.

I knew Wall Street was bugged. I was out-performing her by a mile. It served her right. She may have helped the team win a point or two with a little eyelash fluttering, but I was redefining the entire art of dancing—proving once and for all that guys really were superior to girls.

And, just to make sure she got my point, I bore down even harder. I nodded to the stagehand to pull the rope farther. He obeyed and sent me flying higher. I was breathtaking, doing midair flips, somersaults, everything.

And still I had to show her. "Higher," I motioned to the stagehand. "Higher."

I could tell he was giving it all he had as he pulled down harder and farther.

But it wasn't enough. After all, this was the final battle in the war between the sexes. And it was time to show Wall Street, it was time to show the entire world, who was superior.

"Higher!" I signaled. "HIGHER!"

The stagehand nodded, and with all of his might he gave the rope one last tug. Unfortunately that was the tug that loosened the beam above us. The very same beam that held up that part of the theater . . . the very same beam that now broke from its support and started falling (with a very large portion of the roof following it).

I looked up and managed to squeak out a pathetic "Uh-oh" before it all tumbled down on top of us.

Chapter 9

Team Work

When I regained consciousness, I felt just like one of those famous Egyptian mummies buried underneath one of those giant pyramids—except I wasn't Egyptian or a mummy, and the rocks on top of me weren't exactly a pyramid. (Other than that, it was exactly the same.) The point is, I was buried under more junk and rubble than Mom finds during her weekly forages through Burt and Brock's room.

I was surrounded by darkness. For a minute I didn't know which way was up. Pretty soon I discovered the rope still tied around me and decided to follow it up. I pushed aside all sorts of rock and debris as I started to climb my way out.

Off in the distance I could hear some coughing and choking. And very faintly I heard other voices. I couldn't tell for certain, but they seemed to be shouting something about the President.

I don't know how long I kept shoving stuff off me and pushing up through the junk (time flies when you're having fun), but I finally reached the surface. Then, through the dust and darkness, I spotted my old uniform with the '00' on it.

"Wall Street!" I shouted.

She spun around. "Wally!"

We raced to each other and gave one another a giant hug (though I'd appreciate you not spreading that information around to everybody).

"Are you okay?" I asked.

She nodded. "Looks like everyone got out. Except for the first row where the beam fell."

"The first row?" I cried. "That's where the President was sitting!"

Wall Street's mouth dropped opened. "Are you sure?"

I nodded.

"He must still be under there!"

"Somebody's got to help him!" I shouted.

She shook her head. "Everybody's blocked out. They're all on the other side of that fallen wall."

I spun around and saw that she was right. We were on top of a giant mound of rubble and trapped inside a little chamber. We were closed off from everybody else.

That's when I heard it. ". . . help . . . somebody . . . please help me. . . ."

I turned back to Wall Street. She'd heard it, too. It came several feet below us, buried deep down under the concrete and debris.

"Is anybody there? Please, somebody, help me."

"It's the President," I gasped.

Wall Street nodded.

"What do we do?"

"We've got to save him."

"Us?" I croaked.

"Do you see anybody else around?"

I wanted to explain that, in the interest of national security (and the President's safety), it was better to keep me as far away from the man as possible.

". . . help me . . . please, somebody. . . ."

But Wall Street was right. There was nobody else there to help. Only us.

We quickly dropped to our knees and started digging—pushing chunks of concrete and wood aside, stopping every now and then to listen for the voice.

". . . help me . . . please, somebody. . . ."

Slowly, but surely, we made progress. When we came across big pieces of debris we worked together as a team to lift them. And as we worked together, any memory of the competition between us faded.

The voice below us continued to grow louder and more desperate, "Help me. . . . Please!"

Suddenly Wall Street stopped and pointed. "Right here. He's right under here. I'm sure of it!"

We reached down and grabbed a huge piece of cement. It was more than a little heavy.

"On my count," Wall Street shouted. "One . . . two . . . three!"

We lifted the cement up a few inches and then pushed it off to the side, where it tumbled and rolled down our mini-mountain of dirt and debris.

It was then I spotted him. "There he is!" I pointed to the famous face and silver-gray hair. Unfortunately that was about all we could see of him. The rest was still buried.

"Help me!" he cried as he squirmed and struggled. "Help me! Help me!"

"We are, Mr. President," I shouted. "Just try to relax."

Wall Street and I began digging around him. But we'd only gone a few feet before we discovered the problem. The wooden beam, the very one my rope had been tied to, lay across his chest. It had him pinned.

"Help me!" he cried as he continued to fight against it. "Help me!" Unfortunately all the movement was making the beam shift and press down even harder on him.

He coughed and gasped, "Help me. . . ."

"Mr. President," Wall Street said, "you've got

to relax and stop panicking. You're only making things worse."

But he wouldn't listen. "Help me. . . ." Again he squirmed and again the beam slipped some more, falling even heavier on him. Now he was struggling to breathe.

"Let's try and lift it," I cried.

Wall Street nodded and we moved to opposite sides. We grabbed the giant beam and I counted, "One, two, three. . . ."

We pulled.

Nothing.

We tried again. "One, two, three. . . ."

Ditto in the nothing department. The beam was way too heavy. By now the President was panicking in a major kind of way, fighting and struggling for all he was worth. But he only made things worse as the rock and debris continued falling around him and the beam continued to press down harder and harder. Things were getting serious. At this rate, he would be crushed to death before our eyes.

"What do we do?" I asked Wall Street. "We haven't much time!"

Wall Street scrunched up her eyebrows into a frown. I could tell she was doing some serious figuring.

That was one thing you could say about Wall

Street: she was good at figuring. For years she'd been playing the stock market, hoping to make her first million by the time she turned 13. (Now you know how she got her name.) Anyway, all of that experience made her quite the figurer—especially when it came to math and numbers—though I didn't see how either could do us any good right now.

Suddenly her face brightened. "I've got it! Wally, help me shove that big chunk of concrete there under the beam."

"What's your plan?" I asked as I moved to help.

"This stone will act as the fulcrum point transforming the beam into a lever. By placing it at one third the distance and calculating the estimated weight of the beam in proportion to our combined weight, we should exert a force equivalent to—"

"Never mind," I said. "I'll take your word for it."

But even as we moved the rock into position, the President continued to fight and struggle, bringing more of the weight down onto himself. By now he could no longer talk. In a matter of seconds, he would no longer be able to breathe! Wall Street could do all the figuring she wanted, but if the President didn't relax and stop fighting it wouldn't matter. Someone had to talk to him.

Someone had to take his mind off . . .

Suddenly, I had it. "Mr. President!" I shouted, "Mr. President!"

He barely heard. I dropped down on my hands and knees. Our faces were just inches apart. "Mr. President, have you ever heard any of my super-hero stories?"

He looked at me with such pain that at first I thought he might have. But then he finally gasped, "What?"

"My superhero stories."

He shook his head.

"They're pretty weird. Right now I'm work-ing on this story of Bumble Boy and Shakespeare Guy where Bumble Boy is this half-human half-bumblebee and Shakespeare Guy, well, he's this villain who's trying to make all the world talk like Shakespeare."

He looked at me like I was out of my mind, which was okay by me. At least I had his atten-tion, and at least he'd stopped panicking long enough to listen.

I kept going. I started telling him all about Shakespeare Guy's sinister potion, Bumble Boy's battle with the bats, and how he almost became windshield bug goo—all of this as Wall Street fin-ished doing her calculations and arranging things for the big push. It was kinda cool knowing Wall

Street was busy doing what she did best while I was kneeling beside the President doing what I did best. We were making quite the team.

"Okay, Wally," Wall Street finally called. "We're ready."

I nodded and jumped to my feet just as the President suddenly grabbed my ankle. He was trying to speak. I bent back down to listen.

"What . . ." he coughed and wheezed. "After Shakespeare Guy reaches for the can of bug spray, what . . . happens . . . next?"

I smiled. "I don't know, sir. That's as far as I've gotten. Guess you'll have to stick around a little longer to find out."

He nodded.

"Let's go, Wally!"

I joined Wall Street at the other end of the beam.

"Ready?" she asked.

I nodded.

We hopped on the beam and bore down for all we were worth . . . pushing and jumping. It was hard work, but the beam pivoted on the giant rock, and slowly, ever so slowly, the other end rose off the President's body—only an inch or two, but that was all we needed.

"Hurry and crawl out," I shouted. "Hurry!"

The man groaned and started to pull himself

out. But the beam was too heavy for us to hold any longer.

"Hurry, Mr. President. HURRY!"

"I can't push anymore!" Wall Street cried. "It's too heavy."

"Hang in there!" I shouted. "Just another second. Hurry, Mr. President!"

And then, just before we let go, just before the beam fell back onto the President and crushed him to death, he rolled clear. It smashed down onto the rocks, missing him by less than an inch.

But he was safe. The President of the United States was safe. Wall Street and I looked at each other and grinned. By combining our talents, the two of us had managed to save his life. Not bad for a couple of kids—especially with one wearing a football uniform and the other a pink tutu.

Chapter 10

Wrapping Up

The next morning Wall Street and I stood backstage in our school's auditorium. With all the press people, Governor Makeasplash, and the President sitting in the audience, there was barely any room for the students.

Our 72-hour bet was just coming to an end. Now everyone waited for us to give our speeches to say whether it was harder being a boy or a girl. I threw a glance over to Wall Street. She looked pretty calm. Me too, well, except for my nervous shaking, the hundred gallons of sweat rolling off my forehead, and having to throw up every fifteen seconds. (Other than that, I was just fine.) Fortunately I had Ol' Betsy by my side, so I tried to take my mind off the speech by snapping her on and finishing up my Bumble Boy story.

(When we last left Bumble Boy, Shakespeare Guy was about to rain bug spray on his parade.) He presses the button and the deadly spray shoots out.

PSSSSSSSSSSSS-th.

But Bumble Boy is too fast. He darts this way and that, that way and this, dancing faster than some second grader having to search for a restroom.
Angrily, Shakespeare Guy screams:

"Quit buzzing around thus,
  Try to hold stilleth.
  Thou art making it too hard,
  For me to try and killeth."

Go figure, but for some reason that's exactly what our hero has in mind. He continues flying, and the poet continues spraying until the entire cab is filled with the thick, misty fog...which makes it a little difficult to see out the windshield...which is kinda important if you're driving a tanker truck... which is even more important if that tanker truck is heading down the road

at a gazillion miles an hour...and
there's a hairpin curve just ahead...with
a hundred-foot drop-off...and some very
hard rocks at the bottom. (Other than
that, it's no big deal.)
    And, coincidentally enough, that all
just happens to be the case here.
    "No kiddingth," Shakespeare Guy
mumbles. "What a supriseth."

I paused, trying to ignore the sarcasm of my
villain, and then continued typing.

The truck breaks through the safety
rail and sails toward the deadly rocks
below. Bumble Boy opens his mouth and
with a ferocious cry, yells, "Oops."
    Shakespeare Guy agrees. "I hateth it
when this happensth."
    "Wait a minute," Bumble Boy asks as
they plummet toward the earth, "this
has happened before?"
    Shakespeare Guy nods:

    "In all of his stories,
    Wally ends them the sameth.

His bad guys will loseth,
And the good guys become famousth."

"So what's going to happen next?"
Bumble Boy asks.

"The tanker will crashth,
Spilling out my evil potionth.
You'll wind up a hero,
And I'll become the joketh."

"Excuse me, guys," I type on my laptop. "I
hate to interrupt your little conver-
sation, but can I get back to writing
this story? Bumble Boy has to fly out of
the window before the tanker crashes."
"Wait a minute, Wally," Bumble Boy
says. "Is it true? Do you always have
the good guys winning?"

I hate being quizzed, especially by my own characters. But it was just about time for Wall Street
and me to give our speeches, so I played along.

"Well, yeah," I type. "Good guys win,
bad guys lose. It's like a rule."

Bumble Boy crosses his antennas to form a frown. "So you're saying bad guys are always inferior to good guys?"

"Yeah," I type.

"That they're always less smart, less strong, less——"

"No," I sigh, glancing out at the waiting audience. "Just less good. Now can we get on with the story?"

"What if they turn good?" Bumble Boy asks. "Then would we be equal?"

"Absolutely. Different, but equal."

"Like you and Wall Street?" he asks.

Now I see where he's going with the idea and type:

"Are you saying there's a parallel between what I'm writing in this super-hero story and what I'm living in real life?"

Bumble Boy breaks into a grin. He's pretty smart for a bug.

Suddenly Shakespeare Guy speaks up:

"Hang on for a minute,
   Let's see if I geteth this.

By changingeth my ways,
There's a chance I might liveth?"

"We could work out something," I type.

"Then I quiteth my bad deeds,
'Tis as simple as that.
'Cause the ground is coming quickly,
And I don't want to go splat."

"Okay, fine," I type. "Now can we get
back to the story?"

They nodded, and I resumed my work.

As the tanker continues to fall,
Shakespeare Guy suddenly tells Bumble Boy
he has a change of heart. He no longer
wants to be the baddest of bad guys.
  "Cool," Bumble Boy shouts. "Then I've
got the perfect solution. See that lake
to the right of the rocks we're about to
smash into?"
  Shakespeare Guy nods.
  "Let's try to nudge the tanker over so
it splashes into the water instead."

Shakespeare Guy agrees and throws himself against the side of the cab: Once,
twice, three times...as Bumble Boy
presses his nose against the truck's
side window, buzzing his wings for all
he's worth. It's close, but thanks to
some more incredible writing on my part,
they work together side by side, until
the tanker hits with a tremendous

KER-SPLASH...
GURGLE...
GURGLE...*GURGLE*....

The KER-SPLASH is the truck landing
in the lake. The GURGLE...GURGLE...
GURGLE...is the tanker slowly sinking
to the bottom.

Our dynamic duo pry open the cab door
and swim to the surface. After the
daily minimum requirement of coughing,
gagging, and choking, Shakespeare Guy
cries, "My potion...my potion...."

"Don't worry," Bumble Boy shouts.
"Now that it's on the bottom of the
lake, people will no longer be exposed
to its dastardly effects."

As the two swim toward shore,

Shakespeare Guy confesses, "I don't know
what I was thinking when I invented
something as awful as that."

"Hey," Bumble Boy cries, "listen to
your voice."

"What?"

"You're no longer speaking poetry. The
effects are wearing off. Even on you."

That was the good news. Unfortunately
there was a little bad news too.
Shakespeare Guy is the first to spot
it. "Oh great, check out the fish."

Bumble Boy looks into the water
around him. He sees trout slipping
on tights, bass sporting armor, and
more than one pair of salmon practicing their fencing.

"It looks like the tanker's sprung
a leak," Bumble Boy groans. "It's pol-
luting the lake."

"Then I'll have to hurry and invent
an antidote," Shakespeare Guy cries,
"so we can dump it into the water. Do
you want to help me?"

"Sure," Bumble Boy agrees. "But,
uh, shouldn't we ask Wally?

"Nah, what does he care, he's got
that big speech coming up, remember?"

I stared at my computer screen. I tell you, you give these imaginary characters an inch, and they'll take a mile. I reached back to the keyboard and typed:

"Say, guys! I don't mean to keep butting in here, but are you sure working together is such a good idea? I mean, look at you, you're so different."

"That's the beauty of it," Bumble Boy answers. "With all of our different skills we ought to be able to work together and get that antidote discovered twice as fast."

"He's got a point," Shakespeare Guy says. "Can we, Wally? Can we? Huh? Can we?"

Being softhearted and the type that hates seeing his superhero characters cry, I go ahead and type:

"Sure, knock yourselves out."
The two let out a hearty cheer. And, as the credits begin to roll, they stroll off into the sunset arm in arm. It's a touching ending, knowing that

```
they'll work together and use their
differences to make a difference. (It
would have been even more touching if
it had been my idea. But hey, who am I
to get in the way of a good ending?) The
point is...
```

"Hey, Wally, Wall Street," Sylvia Wisenmouth hissed, "you're on!"

I quickly shut down Ol' Betsy and pulled myself together. Wall Street was getting ready, too. A moment later we walked out onto the stage. Well, Wall Street walked. I did my usual stumbling, tripping, and falling-flat-on-my-face-in-front-of-the-podium routine. (Being nervous makes me kind of clumsy—actually, living makes me kind of clumsy.)

Of course everybody gasped, and the President leaped to his crutches getting ready to hobble for the door in case I pulled a repeat of last night's performance. Fortunately, I didn't.

Wall Street was scheduled to deliver her speech first. I had no idea what she would say, but I could already feel a tightness in my gut as she walked up to the podium.

She cleared her throat and began. "Good morning." After the usual feedback, she continued. "I just want to say that the past three days were hard. I had no idea how hard it was being a guy."

Polite applause.

"In fact, I have to admit it was actually tougher doing guy stuff than girl stuff." There was a long moment of silence. I could see her fidget. She took a deep breath and continued. "This is real hard for me to say, but . . ." She turned to me with a sad smile. "I hereby admit defeat and declare Wally McDoogle the victor. It's true, boys really are superior to girls."

The auditorium went crazy. All the guys were up on their feet cheering. I could see Bruce Breakaface and his bruiser buddies grinning and flashing me the thumbs up. The male reporters and my two Secret Service pals were laughing and giving each other high fives. And, never to let a photo opportunity slip by, the President himself rose to his feet, turned to face the crowd, and gave the victory sign.

When things had finally quieted down (sometime after the year 2063), it was my turn to rise and head for the podium. Someone started to chant, and pretty soon all the guys in the audience were shouting:

"WAL-LY, WAL-LY, WAL-LY!"

I gotta tell you, it was pretty cool. It felt great finally being a hero for once in my life. But before I signed any motion picture deals or began the late night talk show circuit, I knew I had to clear up a couple of things. And I had a sneaking suspicion they were things some folks might not want to hear.

I leaned into the microphone. "My fellow students . . ."

Once again the room filled with feedback, but you could barely hear it over the repeat of all the cheers and applause. It was great. I tell you, I could really get into this hero thing. But when they finally settled down, I knew I had to continue:

"Like Wall Street, I've learned a lot over these past seventy-two hours—especially the differences between men and women."

"You tell 'em, Wally!" some guy shouted. Others laughed and clapped.

I smiled. This was harder than I'd figured. For the briefest second I thought I'd simply accept Wall Street's defeat and keep on being the superstar. But as cool as that would have been, it would have also been a lie.

I cleared my throat, threw a look back to Wall Street, and plowed ahead. "But I've learned something else as well."

I could hear the auditorium get quiet.

"I've learned that different is not better. I've learned that I can do some things better than Wall Street . . . (more applause) . . . and that she can do some things better than I can. . . (dead silence). I've learned that we're not better because we're guys or gals . . . we're just different—with different skills, different abilities, different talents."

I glanced down to the President. He wasn't exactly frowning, but he wasn't exactly smiling, either. I glanced over to Governor Makeasplash. Ditto in her neck of the auditorium.

I swallowed and continued. "And I've learned something else. I've learned that these differences are good. That's how God made us, male and female. And if we work together, as a team, using those differences, it will actually be to our advantage. If we work together, there's nothing we can't do."

It was so quiet you could hear a pin drop (and my knees knock). I took a deep breath and finally brought it to an end. "So, it is with great pleasure, that I also admit defeat, and say that girls are better than boys."

The dead silence grew deader. Nobody clapped; nobody did a thing. I wasn't surprised. I stood there a few more seconds before slowly folding up my speech and turning around. That's when Wall Street leaped to her feet and started racing toward me.

Before I knew it, we were in another hug—only this time the whole world saw it—and this time I didn't seem to mind.

I can't remember all that went on next . . . though I remember Ms. Finglestooper giving some sort of wrap-up speech and Mrs. Permagrin offering cookies at the back of the auditorium. (An event I'd decided to pass on.)

I looked out at the crowd as they rose and started to leave. I knew things were going to be hard the next few weeks. My days, er, seconds of being a hero were over. I doubted the President, Governor Makeasplash, or even the press would be dropping by for any more chats, which was okay because after Bruce Breakaface's meeting, the hospital probably wouldn't allow me to have any visitors anyway.

And still, I knew I'd done the right thing.

"Hey, Wally," Wall Street called from across the stage where she'd been talking to friends. "I've got to write a short story for English. You want to come over to the house later and give me some pointers?"

I shook my head. "I'd love to, but I've got a pre-Algebra test coming up."

"That's all right," she said. "Why don't you help me on my writing, and I'll help you out on your math."

She had a point and I nodded. "That's cool," I said. "Why don't I swing by after dinner?"

"Great." She turned and headed out the door.

For a moment I stood all alone on the stage. I couldn't help noticing how similar this ending was to my Bumble Boy story. How, once we respect each other's differences, we can use them to our advantage.

"Hey, *crunch-munch* Wally?"

I turned around to see Opera waiting at the door.

"Let's *crunch-munch* head on *munch-crunch* home."

"You sure you want to be seen with the all-school moron?" I asked, as I started toward him.

"Sure *burp*, I'm used to it *belch*. Have a chip?"

He offered me his latest bag as we headed out out the door and down the steps—not, of course, without my usual falling, stumbling to keep my balance, and staggering out into the busy traffic, which nearly caused an accident.

HONK . . . HONK . . . SQUEAL . . . SQUEAL . .

CRUNCH . . . MUNCH . . .
CRUNCH . . . MUNCH

"Oh no!" I cried as I peeled myself off a

Mercedes' front grill. "Your chips! Look what I did to your chips!"

We looked down at what was now a bag of smashed potato dust.

"That's all right," Opera said as he scooped up the powder and poured it into his mouth. "We all have unique *gobble, gobble* skills. You were just *scarf, scarf* using yours."

I looked at him and marveled—not only over his incredible eating ability, but over his wisdom. When the guy was right, he was right. I spotted one unbroken chip on the ground, tossed it into my mouth, and the two of us turned and headed for home. Yes sir, Opera was dead on. And what a comfort to know that, as much as we change and grow, some things will always remain the *BELCH!* same.

You'll want to read them all.

THE INCREDIBLE WORLDS OF WALLY McDOOGLE

#1—My Life As a Smashed Burrito with Extra Hot Sauce

Twelve-year-old Wally—"The walking disaster area"—is forced to stand up to Camp Wahkah Wahkah's number one all-American bad guy. One hilarious mishap follows another until, fighting together for their very lives, Wally learns the need for even his worst enemy to receive Jesus Christ. (ISBN 0-8499-3402-8)

#2—My Life As Alien Monster Bait

"Hollyweird" comes to Middletown! Wally's a superstar! A movie company has chosen our hero to be eaten by their mechanical "Mutant from Mars!" It's a close race as to which will consume Wally first—the disaster-plagued special effects "monster" or his own out-of-control pride . . . until he learns the cost of true friendship and of God's command for humility. (ISBN 0-8499-3403-6)

#3—My Life As a Broken Bungee Cord

A hot-air balloon race! What could be more fun? Then again, we're talking about Wally McDoogle, the "Human Catastrophe." Calamity builds on calamity until, with his life on the line, Wally learns what it means to FULLY put his trust in God. (ISBN 0-8499-3404-4)

#4—My Life As Crocodile Junk Food

Wally visits missionary friends in the South American rain forest. Here he stumbles onto a whole new set of impossible predicaments . . . until he understands the need and joy of sharing Jesus Christ with others. (ISBN 0-8499-3405-2)

#5—My Life As Dinosaur Dental Floss

It starts with a practical joke that snowballs into near disaster. Risking his life to protect his country, Wally is pursued by a SWAT team, bungling terrorists, photo-snapping tourists, Gary the Gorilla, and a TV news reporter. After prehistoric-size mishaps and a talk with the President, Wally learns that maybe honesty really is the best policy. (ISBN 0-8499-3537-7)

#6—My Life As a Torpedo Test Target

Wally uncovers the mysterious secrets of a sunken submarine. As dreams of fame and glory increase, so do the famous McDoogle mishaps. Besides hostile sea creatures, hostile pirates, and hostile Wally McDoogle clumsiness, there is the war against his own greed and selfishness. It isn't until Wally finds himself on a wild ride atop a misguided torpedo that he realizes the source of true greatness. (ISBN 0-8499-3538-5)

#7—My Life As a Human Hockey Puck

Look out . . . Wally McDoogle turns athlete! Jealousy and envy drive Wally from one hilarious calamity to another until, as the team's mascot, he learns humility while suddenly being thrown in to play goalie for the Middletown Super Chickens! (ISBN 0-8499-3601-2)

#8—My Life As an Afterthought Astronaut

"Just cause I didn't follow the rules doesn't make it my fault that the Space Shuttle almost crashed. Well, okay, maybe it was sort of my fault. But not the part when Pilot O'Brien was spacewalking and I accidently

knocked him halfway to Jupiter. . . ." So begins another hilarious Wally McDoogle MISadventure as our boy blunder stows aboard the Space Shuttle and learns the importance of: Obeying the Rules!
(ISBN 0-8499-3602-0)

#9—My Life As Reindeer Road Kill
Santa on an out-of-control four wheeler? Electrical Rudolph on the rampage? Nothing unusual, just Wally McDoogle doing some last-minute Christmas shopping . . . FOR GOD! Our boy blunder dreams that an angel has invited him to a birthday party for Jesus. Chaos and comedy follow as he turns the town upside down looking for the perfect gift, until he finally bumbles his way into the real reason for the Season. (ISBN 0-8499-3866-X)

#10—My Life As a Toasted Time Traveler
Wally travels back from the future to warn himself of an upcoming accident. But before he knows it, there are more Wallys running around than even Wally himself can handle. Catastrophes reach an all-time high as Wally tries to out-think God and re-write history. (ISBN 0-8499-3867-8)

#11—My Life As Polluted Pond Scum
This laugh-filled Wally disaster includes: a monster lurking in the depths of a mysterious lake . . . a glowing figure with powers to summon the creature to the shore . . . and one Wally McDoogle, who reluctantly stumbles upon the truth. Wally's entire town is in danger. He must race against the clock, his own fears, and learn to trust God before he has any chance of saving the day. (ISBN 0-8499-3875-9)

#12—My Life As a Bigfoot Breath Mint
Wally gets his big break to star with his uncle Max in the famous Fantasmo World stunt show. Unlike his father,

whom Wally secretly suspects to be a major loser, Uncle Max is everything Wally longs to be . . . or so it appears. But Wally soon discovers the truth and learns who the real hero is in his life. (ISBN 0-8499-3876-7)

#14—*My Life As a Screaming Skydiver*
Master of mayhem Wally turns a game of laser tag into international espionage. From the Swiss Alps to the African plains, Agent 00½th bumblingly employs such top-secret gizmos as rocket-powered toilet paper, exploding dental floss, and the ever-popular transformer tacos to stop the dreaded and super secret . . . Giggle Gun. (ISBN 0-8499-4023-0)

#15—*My Life As a Human Hairball*
When Wally and Wall Street visit a local laboratory, they are accidentally miniaturized and swallowed by some unknown stranger. It is a race against the clock as they fly through various parts of the body in a desperate search for a way out while learning how wonderfully we're made. (ISBN 0-8499-4024-9)

#16—*My Life As a Walrus Whoopee Cushion*
Wally and his buddies, Opera and Wall Street, win the Gazillion Dollar Lotto! Everything is great, until they realize they lost the ticket at the zoo! Add some bungling bad guys, a zoo break-in, the release of all the animals, a SWAT team or two . . . and you have the usual McDoogle mayhem as Wally learns the dangers of greed. (ISBN 0-8499-4025-7)

Look for this humorous fiction series
at your local Christian bookstore.